10 TWISTED

PULP
FICTION

TALES

ALLAN KEVORKIAN

Publisher's Cataloging-in-Publication
(Provided by Cassidy Cataloguing Services, Inc.)
Names: Kevorkian, Allan, author.
Title: 10 twisted pulp fiction tales / Allan Kevorkian.
Other titles: Ten twisted pulp fiction tales
Description: First Stillwater River Publications edition. | West Warwick, RI,
USA : Stillwater River Publications, [2025]
Identifiers: LCCN: 2025911833 | ISBN: 9781965733851
Subjects: LCSH: Criminals—United States—History—20th century—Fiction.
| Swindlers and swindling—United States—History—20th century—Fiction. |
Private investigators—United States—History—20th century—Fiction. | Murder—
United States—History—20th century—Fiction. | United States—History—1945-—
Fiction. | LCGFT: Short stories. | Detective and mystery fiction. | Noir fiction.
Classification: LCC: PS3611.E955 A12 2025 | DDC: 813/.6--dc23

To my wife, Jennifer, a woman of deep religious faith. Your unwavering belief in me has carried me through every venture—from the wild ideas to the solid wins, and even the lemons along the way. Whether I was launching a business, changing careers, or quitting a job—Johnny Paycheck style—you stood by me without hesitation. If not for your steadfast support, my stories wouldn't be read by anyone. I'm endlessly grateful—for you, for your strength, and for the remarkable woman that you are.

CONTENTS

1

FREE LUNCH PLUS A HUNDRED BUCKS

Seattle, Washington – A late Friday morning, September '47. Vincenzo Rossi sat in the dim hush of his squalid third-floor apartment—the type of place that made a down-and-outer feel as if the walls were closing in, only to shake him down for the rent. The paint, faded and chipped, clung tenaciously to the horsehair plaster, similar to an unpleasant childhood memory. The ceiling dripped a slow, steady leak into a rusty bucket. A bare bulb hung from a frayed cord, swinging languidly like a dead man in the game you lose when you can't guess the correct letters.

Thirty-seven-year-old Mr. Rossi was as skinny as a pipe cleaner and just as agile. His receding hairline ebbed, mimicking low tide, leaving behind uneven blotches of wiry black hair clinging to his scalp like stubborn seaweed on dry sand. Pockmarks cratered his sallow face, rough as a gravel lot. His ears, thick and misshapen, jutted out akin to bruised potatoes, adding to the overall impression that life had beaten him with a heavy hand.

The black telephone rattled on the nightstand, its shrill ring cutting through stale air. Mr. Rossi, donned in a dirty white dress shirt, sleeves rolled up, reached for it in the sluggish deliberation of someone not expecting good news.

"Yeah?" Rossi growled irritably.

"Vinny? Vinny Rossi?" came a voice on the other end—crisp and refined, the kind alien to his circles.

"Who's dis?"

"Curt, Curt Sinclair. Your old friend from Broadway High School. Found you in the phonebook."

"Eh?"

"I'm in town all week," the unfamiliar voice imparted, smooth and insistent, reflecting someone who'd never heard the word no before. "Let me treat you to lunch. Piermont's on the water."

The thought of a hot meal internally gnawed at him. The last time he'd been to Piermont's, he'd washed dishes there for exactly two hours prior to receiving the boot. They'd called it "not a good fit." He'd viewed it as being shoved into a sink and told to scrub rich folks' waste products.

"Pally, yuh gots the wrong—" He stopped short and shifted uncomfortably in his chair, eyes drifting to the icebox in the corner, its door hanging open like a welcoming tomb. No ice, not today. At best, lunch would be a mustard sandwich. And now, here he was, getting an invite to a joint where an appetizer cost more than his recent paycheck.

"Ah, what the hell? Free lunch," he mumbled inaudibly, his dented chin lifting away from the transmitter.

"You still there, Vinny?"

Vincenzo Rossi's grin widened sardonically, the cynicism in his inflection mixing with the hollow ache in his stomach. To the mouthpiece, he asked, "What time were yuh thinkin'?"

★ ★ ★

Piermont's on the Water was a kind of haven, where the tablecloths presented as meticulously crisp, and candles softly flickered for ambiance, not for visual assistance. The air smelled of money and fine steaks seared to perfection. Floor-to-ceiling windows framed Elliott Bay, where sunlight danced off the rippling water—the view as curated as the salient clientele.

Mr. Rossi's thin lips hardly moved as he told the puny, silver-haired maître d', "Mr. Sinclair is expecting me."

The maître d' bridled, casting a slow, deliberate once-over, posture stiffening, his gaze tracing the stranger's lopsided mustache and crumpled fedora, cockeyed on his head. Rossi's olive skin looked weathered, like a well-worn leather chair left to die atop a mountain. Ole Silver Fox, the host, sniffed derisively—his expression a tight mask of polite contempt—before nodding at the crinkled suit jacket draped over Rossi's arm.

"Sir, you'll need to put that on."

The establishment's smug elder led Mr. Rossi to a seating arrangement for two, where Mr. Sinclair, impeccably dressed and barely thirty, lounged, his eyes resolutely peering down at a giant-sized menu.

Curt Sinclair's shiny black hair was swept neatly to the left, his boyish phiz handsome, polished; the appearance of a man who never had to fight for a thing in life.

Sinclair glanced upward. "Hey, you're not—"

"Vinny Rossi. Yeah, I am."

In the candlelit room, Mr. Rossi stood behind a crisply tucked-in dining chair, fishing a battered wallet from his pocket. He slipped out a creased cardstock driver's license and let it drop nonchalantly onto the white tablecloth.

Mr. Sinclair picked it up, turning it between his fingers. The edges were fragile and peeling, like an old playing card. In the dimness, his gaze lingered on the date of birth.

"Listen, Mr. Rossi, this is a mix-up. The Vinny Rossi I went to high school with is younger than you."

"Well, yuh made me bus it all the way ovuh here, pal. Yuh owe me lunch."

"You don't own a car?"

"Nope," retorted Rossi, exhaling lazily through his nose. "Just toss uh sawbuck down and be on yuh biz. I'll eat uh-lone."

Using a manicured thumb, Mr. Sinclair exhibited a dismissive "get lost" gesture. Instead of obeying, Mr. Rossi stayed put.

Mr. Sinclair eyed him, sizing him up, then languidly rotated his palm up in a half-hearted invitation toward the empty chair. "I didn't order yet. Have a seat, I guess."

"Yuh still buyin'?" It seemed to be no question.

The suave gentleman's square chin tilted with reluctance.

Over the next five minutes, the two men from different worlds gawked apathetically at the menu, ordered drinks, then lunch.

"So, Mr. Rossi," Sinclair said, elevating a cocktail glass, "what do you do for work? Might as well chat, seeing as we're stuck in our peculiar situation."

"Laborer. Odd jobs. Right now, there's no labor an' no odd jobs, so I'm here wit yuh."

Mr. Sinclair's eyes sharpened with interest as two steaks and baked potatoes landed in front of them. "Mr. Rossi," he remarked, his tone shifting, "don't take this the wrong way, but you look like you associate amongst bad people."

"I am bad people."

There was something serpentine in Sinclair's smirk as he took a sip of his martini. "Having you here might be a blessing."

Rossi's fork stalled midair. "Whatcha mean?"

Sinclair set his glass down, his fingertips lingering on the rim as he leaned forward slightly, his voice dropping intimately. "I'm having problems with my wife."

"That's yuh'r problem," the ruffian replied, chewing on the steak as if it owed him money.

Letting his gaze drift around the restaurant, Sinclair edged closer, tone sinking. "How much?"

"Fuh what?"

"To rub her out."

A pause existed in the air as the two men sat facing one another, the soft glow of candlelight casting shadows over their faces. Sinclair shifted his weight, pushing himself back in the chair, his fingers steepled, the gesture deliberate and composed. His smile was impeccable, masking the cold calculation lurking beneath its surface as he waited for Rossi's reply.

Rossi's chewing slowed as he processed what he'd heard. In a world where one man is always pulling the strings on another, he felt the power shift to his side of the table. He enjoyed making Sinclair wait and knew the answer to his one-word question, but he asked it anyway.

"Who?"

"My wife."

Rossi fumbled his fork, wiped his mouth with the back of his hand. "Yuh uh freakin' cop?"

"Nope. Visiting from Fresno. Used to live here as a teenager." Mr. Sinclair pulled out a wallet and dumped its contents between their meal plates. Rossi's dark, lifeless orbs sifted through the mess: bills, a couple of country club membership cards, a folded hotel receipt. After settling on the letterhead of a Golden State Mutual business card, he snorted. "An insurance salesman, huh? What, yuh gots uh policy wit her name on it?"

Curt Sinclair spat coldly. "She's a louse."

"Uh, grand."

"Deal."

"Half up front."

"No way," rejoined Sinclair, pointing an index finger. "I'll give you a hundred now, then the remaining nine when I write the obituary."

The smooth talker slid a crisp Ben Franklin-inked portrait across the table.

Rossi stared thoughtfully at the big bill for a beat, then palmed it, bearing the resemblance of a card shark. "Alright—but yuh're buyin' me uh-nother steak. I'm starvin'."

"Fine. I'll phone you tonight with more details," Sinclair calmly instructed. "But, before you terminate her, I need to know if she's unfaithful. Her name's

Ava, and I think she's got an old flame living in this town."

"Do I ice the flame too? Dat's extruh."

"Nah."

"How am I supposed tuh know the broad's cheatin'?"

"Tail her a few days. Report back to me."

"Wait uh minute," Rossi scoffed. "Dat's extruh."

"The price?"

"Two hundred uh week."

Curt Sinclair nodded. "I'm only here for a week. I'll add it to the nine." He reached into his suit jacket, then slipped a black-and-white photo across the table. "It's yours."

Rossi smirked, lips cockeyed, eyeing the pretty dame on paper. Then leaning back in his chair, he stuffed the photo into his shirt pocket. "Double-cross me, and there'll be two murders," he warned menacingly.

Sinclair gulped as the color drained from his features. His brow creased, lips pressing into a tight line, a bead of sweat forming at his temple. He quickly peered low, fingers trembling at his waist, steadying himself prior to speaking in a quieter, less authoritative tone.

"Don't worry, I have adequate funds in the bank. And when I get the life insurance check, I'll give you an extra five hundred as a bonus—as long as it's a clean job. Meaning no coppers asking questions.

Has to look like an accident—fewer inquiries that way." Using a fork, Mr. Sinclair toyed with his food and continued, "Murder's too suspicious. And it can't appear as a suicide; there's a clause in the policy."

"I'll make it uh clean accident," assured Rossi. "What if she's not cheatin'? We still killin'?"

"Yes. But I don't want it to happen until I'm ready to return to California. For now, simply shadow her, figure out how you're going to do it, then report back to me before you make a move."

To the approaching waiter, Mr. Rossi barked, "Another steak here. Pronto."

* * *

A day passed. Vincenzo Rossi had the instructions—and a promise. A promise that came alongside eleven hundred bucks, plus an extra five hundred smackaroos if the job stayed tidy. He reckoned agreeing to the free lunch was the best break he'd landed since his pal Tubby got out of the can three months back and coughed up the three hundred he owed him. Rossi blew through that dough in a week, a racetrack and a stripper named Sally claiming most of it.

Rossi took a bus twelve miles south along Route 99 to reach the city of Renton. At Longacres Racetrack, he cashed Sinclair's hundred: twenty-five on Dame's Regret to win, fifteen on Gutter Gold to place, and ten on Loaded Dice to show. Didn't know a thing about the horses; he just fancied the names.

The remaining fifty would be enough to keep the landlord at bay, press a few suits, buy some decent meals, and maybe run around town with a pair of willing, buxom floozies.

Now, it was time for business, time to earn the rest of the pot of gold. He knew the Olympic Hotel well, a landmark in Seattle. The establishment, however, wasn't so well-acquainted with him. He held her photograph up to the sunlight, and his heinie found comfort on a nearby park bench.

Eventually, Ava Sinclair stepped out of the grand dwelling, gracefully mirroring a vision from a dream, if dreams came dressed in silk and walked on heels that clicked purposefully against the pavement.

The redhead showcased a kind of beauty which forced men to forget their troubles and remember life's tasty fruits. Her hair, a deep copper fire, tumbled in soft waves that framed a face painted to perfection—lips a sultry crimson, eyes dark-lashed and enchanting. The emerald dress hugged her like it had been sewn on, one slit at the side revealing just enough leg to have businessmen tripping over themselves. She paused at the curb, adjusted one glove with a deliberate tug, then surveyed the street as if it belonged to her.

Mr. Rossi watched the sway in Ava's hips from his perch, a cigarette burning low between his fingers.

The predator's gaze slowly dragged upon her, hungrily assessing, mimicking a man taking stock of something he could never possess anyway. It would make the sin easier.

Rossi, in his cheap suit and tattered fedora, followed her to the McAlister's Department Store lunch counter. The joint presented as plenty busy, yet no one seemed to notice his shabby attire or ugly, marred mug. Her allure commanded all the attention.

He slid into a phone booth, cracking the door barely a smidge. He wondered what a woman like Ava Sinclair was doing in a place such as this until he heard her tell the server, "I hear you've got the best corned beef sandwich in Seattle." She crossed one leg over the other in a slow, calculated motion—one that didn't go unnoticed.

Rossi sensed he shouldn't have, but he eased onto the stool two down from her, the space between them empty—a sinister invitation. By way of a freckle-cheeked kid, he ordered a coffee, black, and lit up a stick, the smoke eddying idly into the air.

To his surprise, Mrs. Sinclair turned toward him, her gaze unflinching. "Got a spare?" she asked, her voice cocky.

He nudged a cig from a pack, leaving it there for Ava to pluck. His lighter flicked to life, the flame catching as he lit her up.

Letting her see his pockmarked kisser was a mistake, but historically, Rossi thrived on poor judgment.

It became his poison, and fixing it, the antidote. He knew tailing her, going forward, would be a daunting challenge; she'd spot him the second he made a move. However, he was a man of solutions, and this job seemed no different. He'd find a way to complete the task and reap its rewards.

Then Ava Sinclair hit him with it: "So what's to do in this town, anyway?"

He reckoned the ball just bounced squarely into his court.

★   ★   ★

Sunday morning, in Vincenzo Rossi's seedy apartment, the phone jangled—echoing the shrill annoyance of a cheap alarm clock. He let it shriek through four tiny rings, leaning rearward indolently in his creaky chair, two feet on a rusted radiator. Not because he was far from the phone but because he wanted the caller to sweat.

In the middle of the fifth ring, he picked up the receiver, employing a sluggish twist of his wrist.

"Yep," the rogue muttered, cigarette smoke curling lazily out of the corner of his mouth.

The caller on the other end said, "It's Curt Sinclair."

"Yep," Rossi repeated, pretending the words bored him. He stretched for a chipped coffee cup, took a mouthful of lukewarm black sludge, and formed a contorted face.

"Vinny, do you want the money or not?"

A lazy smirk tugged at Rossi's lips. He planted an elbow on a side table littered with old racing tickets and empty pill bottles. "Go ahead, pal. I'm still wit yuh. Yuh ain't callin' from a hotel room, are yuh?"

"No, a payphone."

"Good. Don't trust dem hotel operators. They love tuh listen in, y'know."

"Did you follow my wife?"

"Even betta," Rossi said, scratching his jaw idly, utilizing the wet butt of his cigarette. "Gainin' the dame's trust."

He pinched the bridge of his nose, the cord twisting in his hand.

"Eh?" hissed Curt Sinclair, his voice sharp, like he'd just bitten into a lemon wedge.

Rossi chuckled—a low, throaty rumble. "I think," he theorized, savoring the words, "she digs me."

There was a pause.

"You gawk in the mirror recently, Rossi?"

Rossi snorted, flicking ash crudely onto the linoleum floor. "Gonna let dat one slide, pretty boy."

"Sorry, I'm a tad nervous," imparted Curt Sinclair to the mouthpiece. "So, you actually spoke to her? We don't have a lot of time for you to figure out how you're going to do it."

"I've been givin' her sightseein' tips," Rossi drawled, taking a load off the radiator. "Last one's gonna be Kinnear Park—uh cliff is there, uh quiet spot. Uh little ledge sits maybe twenty-five feet down before the big drop." Rossi continued, "Perfect fuh uh fall. I'll clock her noggin' wit uh rock, give her uh shove, and let gravity do the rest. She'll hit the ledge—dead already—but it'll look like she slipped and cracked her skull on impact. Nothin' suspicious. Coppers know no suicide bird's gonna take such uh short leap. Uh few others've gone over in the same spot—hikers, usually just leg breaks."

Mr. Sinclair's voice softened a notch, as if he was reveling in the idea. "I recall the park from my child-hood. And I dig it. Lug the bloody rock home with you. Exactly how'll you transport Ava there?"

Rossi's sneer traveled through in his voice—coarse and dangerous. "If wifey agrees to a date," he rasped, "I'll take her myself. If she turns me down..." He let the sentence dangle in the air, then added casually, "I'll haul her against her will."

"You can't leave tie marks on her," Sinclair warned, his voice sliding low. "Obvious kidnapping will raise suspicion."

Rossi shrugged effortlessly, even though Sinclair couldn't see him. "Let me try it the easy way. Might do lunch wit her uh coupla times to gain her trust." He stubbed out the cigarette on the arm of his chair, creating another blackened crater in its upholstery.

"She's not gonna agree to get in a car with you," Sinclair cautioned, nervously glancing out of the phone booth's glass. "Thought you didn't own one?"

The fixer snickered, slouching back once more, nonchalantly. "My friend Tubby's got one I can borrow."

"You can't kill Ava until Thursday," Sinclair instructed. "That's in four days. I'm escorting her to a company dinner on Wednesday night; we need to present as a happy couple. See to it she writes down all the sightseeing places you give her on a piece of paper. Make sure that list is in her handbag when you do the deed—it'll appear as a tourist accident."

"Thursday it is," Rossi said smoothly. "The list will be in the bag. Get my money ready."

Vincenzo sat up straight, his mind working on the details, the nascent plan beginning to solidify. *A cliff, a rock, a fall*—it was a simple job. Clean. His deliberations were cold—calculating the next move.

"Keep me posted," Sinclair urged, disrupting Rossi's rumination—his voice firm.

The line went dead.

★   ★   ★

A day later, twenty-nine-year-old Ava Sinclair again perched elegantly at McAlister's lunch counter, the very picture of elegance, draped in danger. A woman who wouldn't cut a fellow an inch of slack.

The classy lady's sapphire-blue suit, tailored within a degree of perfection, clung to her curves, exhibiting an understated power that whispered of wealth and control. A matching hat, tilted at a rakish angle over flaming hair, cast a veiling shadow that deepened the mystery in her dark-lashed eyes.

Her gloves, inky black and ending a smidge below the elbow, were the kind a woman wore when she didn't want to leave fingerprints. Her heels, a glossy navy, tapped softly against the linoleum floor, as if measuring the seconds to something inevitable.

Shoppers hurried behind her, their footsteps a blur as they jostled past, arms loaded with bags of unnecessary purchases, all in a frantic rush, allowing no time for lunch. The noise of their movements filled the air, a constant hum of restless energy.

Suddenly, amidst the chaos, the rough-hewn visage of Mr. Rossi materialized from out of nowhere, encroaching into Mrs. Sinclair's orbit, mirroring a tainted silhouette. He loomed two stools down at first, his presence slimy yet subtle—the sort of thing his kind had a knack for.

When she said, "Oh, you again," he slithered one stool over, bridging the gap—a snake tightening its coil.

"Hi, miss—"

"Sinclair," she cut him off, her tone cool as dry ice. "Are you following me or something?"

Rossi shrugged, his wiry frame shifting inside the ill-fitting suit. "I usually," he fibbed, slouching, "eat here too, but gotta say, I'm surprised tuh see uh dame like yuh chowin' at uh joint like dis."

Ava raised a flawless, arched brow, giving him a

stare so incredulous it could've peeled paint off the walls. "Chowing?"

Rossi flashed a crooked, open-mouthed smile—the kind of teeth which hadn't seen a dentist since America's Depression. "Yeah, yuh know. Grabbin' a bite."

He leaned in just slightly, enough to make it feel intimate and uncomfortable all at once. "I've gots some more local landmarks fuh yuh tuh visit. Write 'em down," he murmured huskily, nodding as if he'd shrewdly handed her a winning tip at the racetrack.

The freckle-cheeked server sauntered over, and Mrs. Sinclair pleasantly ordered, "A cheeseburger, fries, and a Coke."

Rossi mimicked her lofty voice with a chuckle. "Cheeseburguh, fries, and uh Coke." He glanced sideways and, annoyingly, remarked, "Yuh'r uh cheap date."

The comment went unanswered. Ava's cool demeanor didn't falter as she removed her leather gloves from long, sylphlike fingers, reached into her purse, and set a small notepad on the counter. "Go ahead," she snapped, her voice smooth but detached, reminding him his visitation was on borrowed time.

Rossi rattled off a few landmarks, and she kept writing, her manicured fingers as precise as a surgeon's. Finally, he leaned in once more, lowering his voice a notch. "Last one, Kinnear Park. Beautiful scenery. I know it well."

Silence enveloped them.

Kinnear Park, he thought, letting the moment hang in the air. Relishing it in his mind, he was already there—imagining how much pleasure he'd take in killing the bitch, watching her limp body descend. Maybe, initially, he'd have his way with her in the back seat of Tubby's battered car, prior to dumping her shell over the ledge. His lips curled faintly as Red's fatality played out in his brain's sordid theater in full color. The monster understood his compulsion for violence was unquenchable.

She dropped the pencil on the laminate surface and pivoted toward him, steel in her eyes slicing through his twisted reverie, akin to a chilling blade.

Rossi felt his throat tighten, her words choking the air in his windpipe after she asked bluntly, "Is that where my sap of a husband plans on having you throw me off the ledge?"

* * *

Tuesday, Vincenzo Rossi, alongside Tubby Olsen—a man showcasing more chins than the San Francisco white pages—took the Bremerton Ferry across Puget Sound. It became a slow, hour-long ride through slate-gray waters. By the time they arrived at the Viking Dog Track, an unpretentious omphalos for Seattle's degenerate gamblers, the early afternoon sun hung low and hot, painting the circuit in dusty gold.

The two scoundrels leaned over a sagging wire

fence, away from the main crowd. It's where the real gamblers gossiped. The gnarled wooden posts moaned under the weight of Tubby's bulk. He loomed, akin to a big tuna strung up on a fishing boat—heavy, awkward, and somehow still grinning amidst it all. His mismatched suit appeared big enough to cover an adult buffalo. Sweat pooled on his greasy forehead as he rolled today's event program tight in one pudgy hand, then slapped it fiercely against the railing like it'd ripped him off.

"Come on—" he thundered, jowls quivering, "you two dogs!" His roar boomed across the track, drawing a couple of disdainful looks from bettors clustered on the outskirts of the action.

On the dirt course below, eight greyhounds sped past in a blur of taut muscle and frenetic energy, their sleek bodies stretching forward as if chasing ghosts through the bedlam of the crowd's shouts.

Rossi watched them absently, his mind hardly registering the canines' frantic chase. The decorous Ava's slick, perilous voice relentlessly played on repeat in his head.

"Let's reverse the coin. I'll give you five grand to ice Curt," she'd said, her words from yesterday smooth as honey over broken glass.

He recalled blinking—stunned—when Ava first uttered those words. For a person used to holding all the cards, it had been a strange sensation, like having the deck yanked right out of his hands. He could still

feel the way his mouth went dry and how his pulse had quickened beneath his wrinkled shirt.

He remembered responding, "Five grand, huh?" His tone came out gravelly, even rougher than usual. "Yuh always carry dat kinda dough, or do yuh just make promises off the cuff?"

Now, a day later, standing at the fence, his brain worked overtime, calculating. Ava's offer: five grand. Curt's offer: one grand, two hundred to tail, plus five hundred if clean. A hundred already spent.

His fingers curled around the wire, digging into the rusted metal until the tips of his fingers reddened. The physical discomfort barely registered, his focus consumed by his thoughts. It looked to be a no-brainer on paper. Rossi was starting to think he relished this game—Ava's game. One thing he seemed sure of: he couldn't tell Tubby. Tubby would want in, and Rossi wasn't sharing any of it.

"Hey, Ros!" Tubby's hot breath barked, jarring the hitman out of his warped ruminations. "You even payin' attention? My money's on Lucky Lou for the next race. What 'bout you?"

Mr. Rossi gave him a disconcerted squint, then reached into his pocket and pulled out a crumpled one-dollar bill.

"Yeah, place the bet," he dispassionately muttered. "Lucky Lou it is."

But the only racket he really wanted any part of

was the one that wickedly involved him being Ava Sinclair's pawn.

⋆   ⋆   ⋆

Afterwards, at Mr. Rossi's tawdry, barely furnished apartment, the black phone jangled harshly, like a rusty chain being yanked through a gutter. Rossi, dressed in a sweaty white undershirt and black slacks, let it ring, slit eyes aimed at the peeling ceiling, before snatching the receiver on the fourth clatter.

"Yep?" His timbre aired coarse—the grind of a man who'd been chewing nails.

"Rossi, it's Curt. Curt Sinclair." The voice on the other end of the line was jittery—the kind hard to trust. "It's almost Thursday. How's your setup?"

"Too easy," replied Rossi, running a dirty thumb along the stubbled line of his jaw. He then sparked a match to life and dragged in a lungful of smoke. "Wifey's agreed tuh go on uh lil rendezvous wit me. Kinnear Park."

"Figures," Curt Sinclair quipped, sharp with satisfaction—yet not sharp enough to catch the lie tangled in Rossi's scheme. Oblivious to the widening gulf between bad husband and low-level hitman, Curt's voice grew jagged, his irritation bleeding through, as he added, "Told you she's a louse."

The middleman of death let his lips twist into something nasty. "Pickin' her up Thursday, noon. You'll find the list of tourist attractions in wifey's handbag just like we discussed. The bag an' its contents will take the fall wit her. Call me at three dat day wit my dough."

The line clicked dead. Rossi hung up languidly, fingertips lingering on the cradle. Icing the chump couldn't come soon enough. Figuring he'd be indoors for a few hours, he lugged himself to the six-paned window and gaped it a couple of inches, then peeked into his wallet. Curt Sinclair's original hundred bucks had dwindled to an unlucky seven.

Thirty minutes later, the phone jangled afresh, louder somehow, as if it knew what was coming.

"Yep," he growled again, standing erect, spying on the street below, where nobody ever smiled unless they were buying narcotics.

"Vincenzo, it's Ava."

He fancied it when she referred to him by his first name. The lollapalooza's voice dropped a half-octave, the silky cadence slinking through the receiver, thick and intoxicating. It pricked something in him, a deep and dangerous fantasy, which triggered the wrong kind of thoughts. Dark thoughts.

She didn't waste a breath. Ava Sinclair got right to business, speaking like someone who orders murders as their bailiwick.

"Tomorrow afternoon, I'm picking my husband up from a few hours of solo fishing. We're supposed to go on a corporate dinner that evening. You'll be hiding in the back seat. Tie him up, then put him in the trunk. I'll drive to Kinnear Park, and you do to him what he planned on doing to me. I want to witness it. See?"

"Yep. See." There was sarcasm in Rossi's drawl, idiosyncratic for a man of his character.

Ava curtly orated, "After it's done, I'll drive to a pay phone and report the accident. Then we go our separate ways. But I'll give you a grand as we part. You'll have to come to Fresno next week for the rest; it's where my money is. Can't make a withdrawal that big the succeeding day. Also, this keeps me safe at the park in your gracious presence."

A pause stretched—ample enough for Rossi to recline and let the grin spread drowsily across his mug, understanding the last comment was supposed to be wry humor.

"Yuh'r coverin' my expenses fuh busin' it tuh Fresno," he grumbled convincingly, dragging out each word. "An' don't think about double-crossin' me. In my world, this is uh legit covenant, a murd-uh contract. If there's uh debt tuh collect, I could go tuh people uh-bove me fuh help. Seattle Outfit people."

"My word is good, Vincenzo."

The fixer hung up, plopped into a dilapidated chair as the cigarette burned to a nub between two knuckles. The smirk faded, leaving nothing but the weathered lines of his face and sexual impulses—unfit for a Hollywood movie—ticking through his skull, echoing a metronome from hell.

He missed Ava's voice already—that polished veneer masking the soul of a snake. Somehow, that made him want her all the more.

*   *   *

A dark, cloudy Wednesday rolled into town in the manner of a bad debt. Ava Sinclair pulled up at the marina in a gleaming Packard Super Clipper Eight sedan, its immense whitewall tires brazenly reeking of money. The vixen wore a September dress—a rich plum sheath with modest sleeves—and black leather gloves, her red hair neatly coiled in a bun.

She waved to her husband in his casual attire as he stepped off a motorboat, ditching the poles behind, striding smoothly toward the prestigious automobile. It looked like a marriage created in heaven—or was it a semblance? Regardless, Vincenzo Rossi lay curled up in the back seat, biding his time, donned in a suit as wrinkled as yesterday's newspaper.

"Hi, honey," the insurance man greeted, kissing her cheek. "Didn't catch anything."

She eased the car away from the dock. "Well, I'm sure the stint out there was plenty relaxing."

Before Curt could answer, he felt steel press roughly into his neck.

"Don't move uh muscle, Sinclair," the thug snapped.

"Hey—" The steel dug deeper, cutting off his words.

To Curt Sinclair, Mr. Rossi yelled, "Shut the fuck up!"

To Ava Sinclair, Mr. Rossi pointed, barking, "Pull dis sled behind dat uh-ban-dun' boathouse."

They drove around to the old, barely standing structure, then got out—Rossi keeping the gat pressed firmly against Curt Sinclair's nape. He tossed Ava a facecloth and a length of rope.

"Do yuh know how tuh fix uh knot?"

"Yup. Was a Girl Scout."

"Good. Wrap the cloth uh-roun' his wrists first. We can't leave marks—ain't dat what yuh told me, ole Curtie?" The men exchanged unpleasant glances.

As she tied, Rossi kept his heater aimed on the target.

Curt glared at his wife. "Ava, you're in on this?"

"Curt, I don't know the chap. Seems like you do, though."

"Shut up," Rossi growled savagely to both.

Using his free hand, Rossi quickly checked the knot and gave Curt a nudge toward the rear fender, prodding him from behind with the barrel.

"You'll pay for this, dirtbag," Curt hissed.

"No, just the opposite, I'm gettin' paid," Rossi retorted, then yanked out a bandanna and gagged him, effectively stymying any further smart talk.

Expelling a grunt, he pushed Curt Sinclair inside the trunk and slammed it shut. Sliding once more into the back seat, Rossi leaned low. "Ava, drive.

Obviously, I can't be seen; otherwise, what yuh payin' me tuh do falls apart."

They cruised into Kinnear Park, gravel crunching under the tires. Rossi directed Ava to a secluded spot.

"We go on foot from here," Rossi dictated. "The cliff's just past that brush. Give me the keys."

She handed them off, then he popped the trunk—and Curt Sinclair exploded out, kicking Rossi squarely in the kisser. The ruffian hit the wet earth hard. He was halfway to his feet when he froze, staring down the barrel of a no longer bound Mr. Sinclair's Colt.

"How?" Rossi growled.

"Keep a saw," Curt divulged, aiming at Rossi's chest, "and a piece in the trunk, dummy."

Rossi's eyes flicked to his fallen gat on the lawn, but Curt got there first, booting it under the Packard.

Passing his .38 Special to Ava, Curt cracked his knuckles. "Keep the front sights on him. This hood's about to snag a nap."

He reached into the trunk and wrested out a tire iron. Rossi, still on his knees, wiped blood from his lip and flashed Ava a wink, eyes beaming with a bravado, a gambler on the cusp of a reverse of fortune.

"Dat wuz uh big mistake," Vincenzo rasped.

Ava pointed the Colt—on Curt.

*   *   *

Calling on his best friend, Fat Tubby Olsen laboriously trudged up the creaky stairs to Rossi's third-floor apartment, breathing heavily after floor number two. He knocked once, then yelped, "Ros, you there?"

The door hung crooked on its rusty hinges, the residual stench of dead cigarettes seeping through the cracks. No answer.

Tubby grunted and punched the door, talking through it irritably. "I needed you at the track today, pally."

Meanwhile, back at Kinnear Park, under a charcoal sky, Ava kept the .38 Special aimed steadily at her husband as Rossi palm-swept the soil off his knees.

"Don't shoot 'em," Rossi grumbled. "I'll find uh rock. Stick tuh the plan."

The goon bent low to grab his own gat from beneath the Packard, but Curt's shoe brutally bashed into his face once more, sending him back to the dirt. The enforcer staggered to his knees a second time, glaring up at Ava.

"Bettuh let me hold dat," he muttered tensely. "We gotta tie him up again."

Without warning, Ava swung the weapon toward Rossi, her finger steady on its trigger.

"Nah," she uttered, the power surging through her veins.

Rossi blinked stupidly in confusion. "Huh?"

"Walk to the cliff, bastard," Ava commanded Rossi, her voice an arctic wind.

As the fiend glared at her sullenly, Curt snatched up the fallen revolver from beneath the car.

"So, dis is uh fuckin' setup?" Rossi spat, eyeing the weapon in Curt's hand.

"You molested my sister," Ava snarled menacingly, leveling the Colt, her tone high and deadly. "Two years ago. Then she disappeared before the court date. Wendy Evans."

Rossi staggered to his feet, swiping at his bloodied lip. "Yuh got it all wrong," he rasped desperately. "Dat wuz the uh-thuh Vinny Rossi, the one yuh'r husband went tuh school wit."

Curt propped himself against the rear bumper, shaking his head contemptuously. "There was no other Vinny Rossi."

Rossi's visage drained of color. "Cleavuh," he croaked, glancing between them. "She's buried in Rattlesnake Canyon. Get me tuh the cops, an' I'll show 'em where I dug."

"No deal," Ava replied frigidly.

Both husband and wife now had their firearms trained on their foe's trembling form, a queen and a rook closing in for checkmate.

"Tread slowly until there's no more grass, Rossi," Curt Sinclair instructed, his voice forbidding.

Staggering and seething, Vincenzo Rossi shuffled forward, an upwelling of fear twisting inside him, feeling the barrel of his confiscated gun fixed squarely between his own shoulder blades.

When he reached the edge, Curt rammed him, employing a ferocious shove.

The monster toppled over the precipice, limbs flailing wildly, slamming violently onto a jagged ledge twenty-five feet below. He hit the rocks, the sound carrying a sickening crunch.

Rossi groaned, his delivery ragged and broken. "I...can't move my legs...."

Curt moseyed back to the car.

Ava leaned over the edge, hollering down at her nemesis with chilling detachment, "That's the least of your problems!"

A minute later, Curt returned carrying a gas can. Extending an arm without a word, he tilted the container, letting its fluid trickle out, soaking Rossi's half-paralyzed body as it pooled on the ledge below.

Lying supine, Rossi sputtered helplessly like a fish out of water, his wild eyes displaying terror.

Ava struck a match, watching the tiny flame dance on the tip. She held it for a heartbeat, savoring the moment.

"Enjoy hell," she said silkily. "The devil's waiting for you."

She ignited the entire matchbook and let it fly—a burning arc amid the murky sky—landing square on Rossi's belly.

The ledge erupted in an inferno, fire engulfing Rossi in an instant.

To Ava Sinclair, he shrieked his final word—"Yuh

Jez-uh-bel!"—twisted into a guttural wail as his flesh sizzled and blackened. The air thickened with the acrid stench of charred skin.

The couple turned, drifting toward the Packard as the flames raged beyond them—a towering, fiery monument of vengeance, leaving behind nothing but the smoldering remains of a man who'd finally met justice, Sinclair style.

Curt broke the silence. "Well, that only cost a hundred bucks, a free lunch, and a gallon of gasoline."

Ava slipped into the driver's seat with a faint smile. "Speaking of grub...no more lunch counters. Let's do Piedmont's."

Curt nodded. "Piedmont's it is."

2

THE BOOKS

On a clear September 1947 Wednesday morning, the kind of day that makes the air taste clean, forty-year-old Michele Cappabianca settled into a bus leaving suburbia. He owned a car, but the Pontiac was a gleaming late-model beauty, and he felt safer keeping it tucked snug in his driveway. The 'burbs faded behind him, their quiet streets a universe apart from the grind of bustling downtown Providence. The fifteen-minute ride ticked like a slow hand on a clock as Mr. Cappabianca, flaunting his favorite woolen plaid flat cap over a chrome-dome skull, watched the city draw closer.

The former U.S. Navy torpedoman—Mike, as his American peers referred to him—was a second-generation Italian immigrant who prided himself on his Vieste, Italy, genealogical roots and his artistic painting. Mike's illustrations, along with three daughters, kept him sane since his wife suddenly passed away a year prior. Now widowed, women might best describe him as a non-threatening type—one who practiced gallantry.

The uniformed driver stopped at the majestic Loew's State Theater. Five-foot-eight Mike exited the transit bus and stood facing the playhouse's picture windows, admiring the screaming-for-attention theatrical posters that he had created. Condensation escaping the sidewalk grate below his feet clouded both lenses of his thick, black-rimmed glasses. He fancied the haze; it softened his view of a world that had given him twelve months of pain.

Mr. Cappabianca headed to his independent art shop, the Atlas Sign Company, around the corner from Loew's State. He unlocked the door of the narrow storefront and lit a cigarette. The place housed several unfinished projects, such as advertising signs, department store ads, and sketches of future theater concepts. Older handiworks of past years were displayed as high as the lofty walls would allow. Mike, wearing a white dress shirt and a maroon apron, got to work.

As Mike sketched an image for the upcoming *Iceman Cometh*, college students attending Rhode Island School of Design filtered in and out of the signage den like curious cats.

He did not mind sporadic interruptions; the students seemed to be fascinated by his designs in a schmaltzy kind of way. At 3 p.m., the glass door gaped and the bells attached to it jangled. The artist looked up, then saw his slightly pudgy sister, Roselyn. As she held it ajar, three young girls, all under ten, scampered inside the studio like they were visiting Santa. All together, they hollered, "Papa, Papa!"

Mike released the brush. A barrage of hugs followed, bouncing off his breadbasket. A broad smile tugged at the corners of his lips, his face softening as he enveloped his little treasures in his arms.

Mike's plump-cheeked tiniest daughter, Maria, whose head was covered in a pink bonnet, grabbed the paintbrush. Paula, the middle sibling, owning a crown coated in curls—some brown, some blonde—grasped her arm and scoffed, "Put that down, silly; it's not a toy."

Roselyn's rugged voice boomed, akin to a foghorn, "Michele, I brought you a sandwich."

In a state of exhilaration, Mike ate beside his family. When he finished, his eldest, short-haired daughter, Lucia, animatedly imparted, "Papa, Aunt Roselyn is taking us shopping at Shepards."

He chuckled. "Whenever Auntie takes you kids into that department store, one of you gets lost." The girls only knew their Papa's voice to be genial.

"Not today, I promise," assured a full-faced Roselyn, casting a countenance of certainty. "Please try to pick the lasses up by seven."

Mike nodded his bald head, appreciating the

convenience of having a sister living next door to his house.

The four females departed, and once again, the scene was quiet. Mike worked and smoked. At 6 p.m., bells chimed. Escorted by the late afternoon air, an elderly gentleman strolled in, sporting a gray suit and black hat.

Mike stayed in a sitting position, stroking his brush. While maintaining his focus on the nearly completed theater poster, he politely announced, "I'll be available in a minute."

The man lingered there, his onyx eyes unblinking. He waited thirty seconds, then, airing a foreign accent, impatiently greeted, "Michele.'"

The elder's advent made Mike jump up as if he had just sat on thumbtacks. "Don Lorenzo!"

The senior executed a mini bow. Mr. Cappabianca grounded his cig.

Their conversation resumed in Italian. "I didn't realize," Mike said, edging inward, "it was you."

"Relax, Michele, I had the fortune of passing by this district." The men hugged one another.

"What can I do for you, Don Lorenzo?"

"Michele, I'm hiring you to make a sign for my used lamps business." The man many feared handed Mike an envelope. "Here are the instructions."

Mr. Cappabianca, a man aware of the whispers of the old neighborhood and what unscrupulous activity went on in the rear room of Mr. Lorenzo's staged establishment, felt his knees weaken.

He swiftly peeked and noticed a hundred-dollar bill—triple his normal rate. "Thank you, Don Lorenzo," he muttered, his voice low and respectful. "I'll have the sign ready by Saturday."

"Excellent."

The grandfatherly figure turned to the avenue, but when he pivoted back, Mike grew uneasy. Resembling a Great Gray Owl, the man shrewdly looked about, sizing up the painter's circumstances. Soon, Don Lorenzo resumed, "Michele, I wanted to know if you reconsidered storing our books in your shop's basement. We need a safe spot." Before Mike could reply, the geezer rubbed his snaky fingers together, performing a money gesture, then pitched, "It can give you a better life."

Perspiration beaded at the nape of Mike's neck as he took Don Lorenzo's words and his hand signal as a threat to his health. Subjected to being pestered about it several times in the past, he gave the same answer: "I'm really not comfortable doing it, Don Lorenzo. I'm sorry.'"

"Don't be sorry, Michele. Kindly say hello to your father, Nicola."

And my father warned me never to accept the offer, the forty-year-old mused.

Following a minute of small talk, Don Lorenzo's

departure echoed a cool breeze blowing across a meadow of dandelions.

Mr. Cappabianca flicked off the light switch, leaned right, and stared out of one window, his silhouette etched in the dim background. The city landscape had transformed into gray, as if the life had been sucked out of it. The artist's pulse pounded. The rattling in his chest cavity masked the calm façade he attempted to preserve.

*　*　*

A day later, Mike sat on a wooden stool, smoking, and began laboring on Don Lorenzo's advertising sign. He removed various brushes from his apron and started brainstorming an outline of various lamps. The door jingled, but Mike continued his work of art.

A fragrant scent soon permeated his nostrils. The widower encountered a shapely, mature brunette, close to thirty, who was peering skyward at his theater posters created in years past.

Her face featured high cheekbones, narrow, arched eyebrows, and a cute button nose. She wore a sequin pillbox hat and a long, red, glitzy dress that almost reached her black spiked heels. Mike dropped the brushes quicker than Curly jumping into a horse's watering trough after Moe lit his pants on fire.

His baby blues goggled as he coughed out tobacco smoke. He straightened his posture, smoothing his apron with a crusty hand, stiff from dried paint. "How can I assist you, miss?"

She rotated her head, and Mike beheld dazzling, almond-shaped, close-set eyes in the midst of a seraphic façade. The hazel color made him think of a balcony view with two coffee cups sitting side by side, steaming in the morning light.

"I happened to be walking by," she said, "and the biz piqued my curiosity. I've always had an interest in art." Her tone aired affable, voice a soprano.

The artist gave her a little tour, which may well have lasted all day, as far as he was concerned. The voluptuous woman introduced herself as Veronica and posed plenty of questions, a few of which were personal. Mike explained how he had recently lost his wife to cancer. Aware that his handsomeness trumped his baldness, he straightforwardly asked, "Are you single, Veronica?"

"Currently, yes," she unabashedly revealed.

His jaw locked; he was hypnotized by her attractiveness. Displaying a feline's grace, she snatched a paintbrush from the aisle, ripped a section of scrap paper off a white pad, and scrawled "HN1-6090" in looping ink. Veronica conveyed nothing else. Swiveling on a dagger-sharp heel, she paraded toward the exit, whimsically teasing and drowning him in a lake of mystery.

After three hours, he could no longer hold out.

He dialed Veronica's digits and fell deeper into the spider's web.

*   *   *

Friday night, at the populous Hi Hat Club, they danced off supper. Mike hadn't relished a jazz band this much since before the war, and the last time he remembered wearing a tie was at his wife's funeral. At 10 p.m., sitting in a phone booth, he dialed his sister, Roselyn.

To the mouthpiece, he implored, "Roselyn, please, can my girls sleep over your house tonight?"

Via the receiver, he heard, "Mike, they're already asleep. Enjoy your night." So, he did.

Below an abbreviated dress, Veronica's heels clacked on the pavement as he gentlemanly walked his date to her apartment. Neon lights glared in the distance. The woman's digs lay just four blocks west of his studio. Under an awning of the six-story structure, he planted a goodbye peck on one cosmetically blushed cheek. Veronica lingered at the threshold and watched the tender figure who had just courted her walk distantly to the main avenue.

At a desolate Washington Street bus stop, Mr. Cappabianca glanced at his timepiece. The hands crept toward 12:50 a.m., a grim reminder that the night was waning. The final outbound bus crawled along, ten minutes away from picking up one lone fare: a solitary being lost in the city's dirty secrets.

Mike dug inside a pocket, retrieved a wallet, and counted—then recounted—three five-dollar bills. *Jeez,* he reflected internally.

Meanwhile Veronica entered the lobby of her apartment. A six-foot-two, lanky, hatless man with lubricated black hair, possessing a mug like a Halloween mask, loomed and smoked a Chesterfield. He wore a crisp blue pinstripe suit. She looked up.

"D'yuh think it's a little late?" he growled, sinking sharp fangs through the cig. His voice sounded cartoonish.

"Frankie," she replied deviously, "he's eating out of my hand."

*   *   *

Saturday morning, Mike motored his prized possession—a '46 Pontiac Streamliner—into the city of Providence, Rhode Island's most populated area. He parked on Croom Street in a section known as Shoo Fly. Unlike his, the sparse automobiles in the small village appeared outdated. The landscape consisted of numerous identical, extremely dilapidated three-decker houses, all in immediate proximity to one another. Many were abandoned, including his former childhood home. When he'd returned home from the war, he had helped his parents move out of the dwelling.

Wearing his favored plaid cap and a white dress shirt, he settled his buttocks on the Pontiac's passenger-side fender. Reminiscing about his pauper-boy childhood, he visualized his ten-year-old self throwing a crude baseball to a freckle-faced boy swinging a broomstick handle in an undeveloped plot of crabgrass. Mike recollected chanting, "You can't hit me, I'm Babe Ruth." The field was now infested with piles of discarded wood. When the ritual grew tiresome, Mr. Cappabianca left Shoo Fly, content at where life had taken him.

To whet his appetite, Mike headed to his subsequent stop: a predominantly close by Italian neighborhood called Federal Hill. On both ends of the thoroughfare, he passed vendors peddling produce, cured meats, cheeses, olives, seafood, and bread, all lined up for nearly half a mile. Most drove older-model, flat-roofed, gas-powered trucks, but among them were a few less sophisticated hucksters operating horse-drawn wagons. He had cannoli on his mind. He left the bakery with a small white box of delights, cupping one in his hand and stuffing portions into his mouth gauchely.

His final destination was a smaller-scale Italian neighborhood called Silver Lake. On Pocasset Avenue, he rolled to a halt in front of a seedy little shop called Second Glow. Mike was well aware that it served as a front to launder street money and create bogus payrolls. Vendors and anyone else holding a quarter of a brain knew not to park near the mock used goods company. He carefully transported Don

Lorenzo's sign, not letting it scrape the cement. *Why spend so much on a sign?* he asked himself.

Proximal to the storefront, on the sidewalk, two goons sat rearward in slender banquet hall chairs, taking notice. A third goon, perched in a second-floor window, threw a lit cigarette earthward at the two henchmen. The signal assured that someone was watching their backs. One seated goon, sporting a feathered cap with its brim tilted skyward, rose. The hooligan cautioned, "Hey, we're closed—you can't—" then quickly returned to a surveillance position. "Oh, hi, Mike."

"I'll just be a few minutes, Charlie."

The two ruffians allowed him to pass. A different man might have been filled with slugs. The assassin in the bird's nest lit up a new cig.

Mike's intention had been simply to deliver his artwork, but a lady named Veronica had stimulated his zeal to the point where it became impossible not to dream of countless sexual fantasies. Presently, he needed more dough than a sign painter had the ability to earn. Mr. Cappabianca entered the shady emporium, filled with dusty relics fit for movie props and no customers.

A burly enforcer was stationed at a small desk; something sullen seemed etched upon his kisser. Outsiders, such as Mike, understood that even if you could get past the first three sentinels, you still would not reach Don Lorenzo easily. The fat fellow offered graciously, "I'll take that, Michele." He inspected the sign. "Stupendo, Michele." The artist wondered why Fatty's breath stunk like fried onions.

The men conversed in Italian, their words slinking through the smoky air like shadows in a dark alley. The obese bodyguard patted Mike down from head to toe, checking for anything that might go bump in the night. After the frisk, he was sent to a secluded office. The room had a chill to it, mimicking a butcher's freezer, a place where some men had ventured but never returned. Don Lorenzo sat, garbed all in black, a crooked grin broadcast across the top echelon's wrinkled phiz. A phiz that could silence you in one glimpse.

In the office, more Italian dialogue transpired. At the end of their conversation, Don Lorenzo told him, "Michele, an associate will drop off a stack of books every evening before you leave your shop, and they'll be picked up every morning when you start work. We'll hide them in the cellar. Don't worry about Sundays. You'll be compensated weekly. Never open the books, Michele—never."

"I understand."

"An additional thing, Michele," Don Lorenzo gravely forewarned, pointing across the desk. "Once you agree to this, there is no turning back."

All he could think of centered around Veronica. "Yes, Don Lorenzo."

The two men stood. Don Lorenzo kissed Mike on

one cheek and stuffed a wad of cash into the dupe's pants pocket, one that could have easily choked a donkey. Mike was no longer an outsider, or so he thought.

★ ★ ★

Monday at closing time, as he started packing up, the door opened, and, as always, the three little bells tied to it jangled. A gangly man, six inches taller than Mike, strode in, lugging a box containing a stack of books that resembled journals. His strides were long and purposeful, like a cheetah's, each step a reminder that escaping him would be a daunting challenge

The visitor sported a starched, cream-colored suit and light brown wingtip shoes. As Mr. Cappabianca peered up, he thought the fop's face reminded him of the shark mouths officers had ordered him to paint on Navy airplanes when he wasn't in combat.

Shark Mouth didn't bother with an introduction. "Show me to your basement," he demanded, his eyes narrowing slightly, as if testing Mike's resolve.

Mr. Cappabianca did not require an introduction. The man's name was Francisco Carlino, younger than Mike and certainly no stranger to local newspaper headlines. Thugs on the street tagged him Frankie Carz because of the way he flaunted himself around town in Lincolns and Cadillacs. He carried a distinct scar across his chin, and the artist could only wonder how he had obtained it.

Mike said, "Follow me."

During the brief visit, the guest lacked the Italian warmth Mike was accustomed to feeling. When Frankie egressed, he thought, *Thank goodness.*

The willies Mike had sensed were long gone as he climbed the steps to Veronica's apartment building. From there he wined and dined her for the third time in four nights, expressing no regard for his sister Roselyn, who had reamed him out two hours prior on the telephone for such insouciance in not coming to pick up the girls again.

Under the table at the lively supper club, he tenderly placed one hand on Veronica's nylons. Using her spindly, polished fingers, she lifted up his hand and pushed it aside.

"Not here, Mike," enunciated Veronica sternly. "Not now."

"I'm sorry," he murmured.

Deep in a dingy nook, a man took notice. Frankie Carz lit up a cigarette, a scowl cast upon his tortured mug.

★   ★   ★

At 10 a.m. on Tuesday, Mr. Cappabianca exited the bus and wearily stepped onto the curb, ready for another day of drudgery. Before he reached the door, he was intercepted by a face that hadn't cracked a smile in years. Frankie Carz, dressed in a suit stiff enough to stand on its own, motioned with a tilt of his scarred chin, for Mike to follow him to the corner.

An unmarked burgundy delivery van sat in the alley adjacent to the shop.

"Paint it," barked the criminal curtly, handing Mike a key ring supporting one key.

"Huh?"

"I don't stutta."

"The whole thing?" Mike questioned, confused.

"No, dummy! Paint the doors and side. Write 'Keystone Art Supplies.'" Frankie stared deep into Mike's uneasy eyes. "Make it look legit."

Mike wedged his finger below his cap and scratched his head.

"When we drop the ledgers off," Frankie said, directing his thumb toward the storefront, "we're gonna use the van. Less conspicuous. *Comprendere?*"

Mr. Cappabianca nodded his head, and the men advanced inside. Frankie retrieved the books via the basement and left. Once again, he sensed tranquility.

At 4 p.m., he made a phone call. "Veronica, it's Mike."

"I know." The voice on the opposite end of the line felt cold to him, as if someone lurked at her periphery.

"Can we meet for dinner?"

"Um...okay."

"Seven o'clock, the usual joint," pitched Mike enthusiastically.

"I...I guess."

Mike descended the stairs to the basement, oblivious to the situation. The poor soul pondered, *My money will get her reinterested.* He decided to work on inventory to occupy his mind elsewhere. While he toiled in the understructure, he turned on the radio and began listening to the Yankees game. Mel Allen's voice thundered through the Bakelite device's single speaker. Two hours passed, and, at closing time, as expected, the door jingled.

"Mikey?" The painter recognized the cartoon-like voice, originating from above, as belonging to a man he didn't fancy, any more than he did being called "Mikey."

"Down here."

Frankie slowly descended the stairs. Mike attempted small talk. "DiMaggio's got two home runs."

"Who gives a shit, Mikey?"

Mr. Cappabianca's blood boiled inside but he remained reticent on the outside. He continued his inventory while Frankie lifted up a piece of wood where some utility valves slept. He plopped the books in the hole and put a wooden crate over them.

Frankie swaggered by, eyes never meeting Mike's, as if he were already dismissing him as insignificant. Mike lowered the radio's volume as the racketeer ascended the cellar steps. When the door upstairs jangled, he tuned the dial to a jazz station and blasted the song to celebrate Frankie's unceremonious departure.

Any moment of euphoria would be a blessing. Unfortunately, he could not relax. He eyeballed the wooden crate, walked to it, and kicked it with his foot. *What the hell is in these books?* he pondered.

Unbeknownst to Mike, Frankie failed to leave. The tinkle was a decoy. Mike's sonorous music drowned out the hood's footsteps one floor up. Once at the unsecured sublevel door, the ruffian got on his belly and, headfirst, slid down the stairs like the snake many people might agree he emulated. Frankie descended enough for his ugly face to poke out past the wooden partition that bordered the staircase.

Mike would have had a surprise if he had pivoted around, but he did not. Instead, he flipped pages and inaudibly whispered, "Judges, councilmen, city workers, all on the take." He examined the second book. "Loansharking!"

Frankie had observed enough. Utilizing his muscles, he pushed his body upstairs. As he became erect, he used both hands to brush off his suit. On his way out, he laughed and jangled the bells further than necessary, as a cryptic message. Next, he skulked away from the shop.

Mike heard it and ran upstairs, finding no one. The artisan dashed back downstairs and hid the criminal syndicate ledgers.

The door jingled again, and once more he barreled up the stairs.

Tall black boots authoritatively led a towering

red-headed man in a state police uniform toward an out-of-breath Mike.

"Hi, pal," the thick fellow said haughtily, "saw you were open later than usual. Just making sure everything was okeydokey."

Mr. Cappabianca recognized the trooper as Colonel Hagen, an individual who occasionally hired him to paint state police signs at—regrettably for Mike—a lowball rate. Mike also knew of the colonel's reputation as a stalwart who could not be bought by the underworld.

"Yes, Colonel, I'm finishing up."

"In a week or so," the colonel announced, "we're going to need some signs for the new barracks. We'll furnish the diagrams beforehand."

"Sure, Colonel, thank you." Mike really wanted to say, *Lucky me*.

Across the avenue, at a deserted, ratty little coffee shop for broken souls, one lone mobster sat at a long table facing the window. Like a hawk watching a squirrel, Frankie Carz attentively spied the policeman's withdrawal from the studio. A grimace twisted his shark-like face as he drew his brows together. "Bastard!" exclaimed the gangster to an audience of none, the cadence a meager growl, coated in venom.

⋆   ⋆   ⋆

On Atwells Ave, at a quaint place called the Villa Cucina, Mike, donned in a dress shirt and tie, perched on a barstool. Veronica was an hour late. The maître d', garbed all in white, approached the bar for a third time.

The lonely spirit shook his bald head. "My date's a no-show, Anthony." Bracing himself against the bar to support his elbows, he rested two hands on his mandible. "Give my table away," he muttered abstractly. Resigned, he requested another highball cocktail, and then another. When his bladder filled, he plodded to the men's room.

Alongside Mike, at the adjacent urinal, surfaced a miscreant he preferred to avoid. It happened to be a troublemaker he had attended grammar school with, notorious on the streets, named Johnny San. There were additional vowels in his last name, but nobody seemed to remember them.

Johnny San stood at five foot five, three inches shorter than Mike. He wore a black leather jacket and a porkpie hat atop his naturally puckered facade. While Mike was relieving his bladder, Johnny San, doing the same, divulged, "Just lettin' ya learn dat the dame you're waitin' for is Frankie Carz's lassie." The shrimp's street slang voice squeaked like rusty hinges.

Returning to the dimly lit bar, Mike felt destroyed. He drank until he could barely open his baby blues. Stumbling with each step, he made it to the inner-city bus stop by 1:10 a.m. He glanced at his watch with bloodshot eyes, but it looked fuzzy. The clock on a department store appeared clearer. He had missed the last outbound ride.

Mike staggered down the misty boulevard—his pace as aimless as his judgment. Outside Veronica's red-brick apartment complex, inebriated from alcohol, he teetered purposelessly like a puppet controlled by entwined strings. Eventually, he unsteadily trudged to his sign shop. His hands went into the pockets of his coat for the shop keys, but his foggy brain discerned the coat was not on his body—he'd left it behind, along with whatever self-respect he had remaining.

It's on the barstool, he remembered.

He searched his pants pocket and found the key ring for the van Frankie had ensconced in the alley. After three botched attempts to find the keyhole, Mike finally unbolted the passenger door and sat in that seat, smoked a cigarette, and rifled through his wallet. The clump of bills Don Lorenzo had given him dwindled to single digits.

Now, he just wanted sleep. He scaled the upholstery and curled up in the rear of the delivery van, not realizing he had left the passenger door unlatched. Within five minutes, his pounding head surrendered to dreamland.

★　★　★

Wednesday, 10:15 a.m., Frankie waited, but there was no Mike, so no books. Frankie's ears detected heels clacking on the sidewalk. Veronica emerged in a V-neck checkered dress.

"Whatcha doin' here?" inquired the thug rudely.

"Giving goofy Mike a piece of my mind. He came by my apartment at one thirty in the morning and tossed sticks at my window."

Frankie gawked at the dark storefront. As he did, the environment became more crowded with pedestrians.

"Talk over here," he directed, pulling her sleeve forcefully until they reached the alley.

The conversation had been planned for the alley, but Frankie noticed the unlocked door of the van. He ordered, "Climb in." She obeyed.

Voices in the front seat caused a late sleeping Mike to unseal an eye. He curled his frame close and listened.

Frankie began, "I'm goin' to eliminate this guy."

"Oh."

"I caught him," Frankie divulged, "peekin' in our business."

"Does your boss know?"

"No. Don Lorenzo might give him a pass. He loves Mikey for some reason."

"I can't think of one," she sneered.

Frankie leaned against the steering wheel and spoke to the windshield. "Why would Don Lorenzo bring this guy in?"

She shrugged.

"Don Lorenzo asked me to nonviolently persuade him to stash the records," Frankie resumed. "So I used you, but he's not one of us. Mikey's soft, and he's already squeakin' to the cops."

Through lustrous lips, she laughed maliciously. "Let me shoot him. I'll agree to one more date and blast him."

The mobster grinned. Frankie fancied Veronica a lot more than he had five minutes ago. Behind the front seat, Mike held his breath, paradoxically fancying Veronica a lot less.

"Sure," Frankie willingly conceded. "You can do my dirty work. Don't mess it up. It has to be done in his heap, somewhere secluded. We leave the remains there."

She applied more lipstick, then cunningly smiled. "Yes, darling."

Consternation triggered tachycardia, rattling inside Mike's thorax.

"I will tail his wheels in my Caddy," disclosed Frankie deviously, "and pick you up when it's done."

"Yes, darling," she said once more.

The sinister couple exited the van. Mr. Cappabianca heard Frankie say, "I'll have to come back here in an hour to snag the books. Where is this bum?" Simultaneously, the doors shut.

Blast him? Who's going to raise my daughters? thought Mike, shivering in fear.

*   *   *

He arranged another date, one laced in danger. "Fetch your ride this time; we'll go parking at India Point," she purred over the phone line. Unbeknownst to her, it was on a level playing field. Mike knew the score and had the rules memorized.

The September evening aired cool, appropriate for his feelings. As expected, in the shadows, he saw Frankie's car around the corner from Veronica's apartment complex—a coiled boa constrictor bearing deadly intentions

The painter climbed out of his Pontiac and slunk low next to Frankie's opulent white Cadillac. Mike, crouching, unscrewed the valve stem cover off the Caddy's rear passenger tire, while an incognizant Frankie fiddled with the convertible's radio. Subsequently, he inserted a matchstick, and the outcoming air expelled a slight hissing sound. He crawled on his knees along the frame and performed the same trick to the driver's rear tire.

As Mr. Cappabianca pulled his automobile up to the façade of the edifice, she was waiting for him, dressed to kill in black. Veronica's dolled-up face gave his right cheek a kiss. A Judas kiss. Frankie pursued the duo, but, unfortunately for him, two tires slowly deflated. Mike directed his vehicle outside the city limits.

Nudging his shoulder, she said, "Hey, this isn't the route to India Point Park."

"Going to East Providence instead; I recall a place."

She swiftly rotated her head and glanced through the glass.

"What are you looking for?" he asked.

"Um...nothing special," she replied.

In a remote area unfamiliar to her, Mike braked his prized possession. In the murkiness, they conversed superficially as the windows fogged up, reminiscent of a foreign movie's dream sequence. She casually yanked out a revolver and leaned her spine against the interior panel of the passenger door, burrowing a barbed heel into his thigh.

"Don't do it," he pleaded, bug-eyed, gawking down the mouth of the barrel.

"Why go to the cops, Mike? You know, the books."

"You crazy? The trooper is a customer at the shop."

"Well, I won't," she caustically revealed, "tell Frankie that part. Goodbye, Mike."

She engaged the trigger as Mike swiped up his right hand, making contact below her wrist. The bullet missed him and shattered the driver's side window. The gun fell to the floor. Veronica's handbag was still open. Abruptly, she pulled out a folding knife and deftly opened it.

Mike grabbed her neck as she aimed the blade at his chest. By misfortune's grace, the knife sank into his right shoulder. He screamed in agony. Around her neck dangled a black scarf. His thoughts did not dither. Employing both hands, he applied strong inward pressure against her neck, wielding the scarf while she clawed at his face.

The clawing gradually attenuated. When her cheeks turned purple and her arms became lifeless, he stopped.

He gazed out the shattered window, but all he saw was darkness. He dislodged the cutting tool from his deltoid, grunted, then dropped it on the seat next to the corpse. His hands trembled, analogous to someone typing a letter minus a typewriter. Despite the trembling, he managed to light a cigarette.

What have I done? Mike reflected.

After five minutes, he unlocked his trunk. He had hoped the night would not lead him there, but that was where his shovel rested. As he dug the shallow grave, headlights rapidly approached. He crept beyond a bush, hearing the interloper's engine rumbling. Mike knew he had not peed his pants since age three, but now felt like a good time.

Through the tangled bush, he observed a jalopy prowling for a private spot. The teenage lovebirds encroached within thirty feet of a hidden Mike. They pinpointed his car, exited, and found an adjacent lawn, blissfully unaware of the man crouching in the shadows whose life had become twisted like a deranged pretzel.

Can't bury the bitch here, he reckoned internally.

He absconded from the desolate park, hauling one dead gal and a shovel in his trunk.

As he returned to the congested city, his keen eye caught Frankie's grandiloquent Caddy slouched on the side of the road like a wounded beast. The outlaw was displaying his backside and violently banging his fists on the hood, loud enough to chase a mouse out of an alley. Three tires were inflated, the fourth a goner, meaning the roughneck had only one spare. Mike had calculated that part well. Frankie never spun around, too preoccupied with his tantrum. Mike kept proceeding, his countenance aghast.

Cruising the city of Providence with a stiff lying supine in the trunk caused Mike's nerves to twitch. Considering this and his extreme shoulder pain, his Pontiac began to swerve erratically. A squad car got up on his tail.

He heard, "Are you in control of your vehicle?" blaring out of a speaker.

Mike's left hand executed a thumbs-up sign outside the busted window, which simply presented as an open window. The cruiser positioned itself alongside him. Two coppers looked hard. Mike put both hands on the wheel, keeping the '46 Streamliner in his lane.

The officers missed his bloody shirt and the beads of sweat pouring down his forehead because ten seconds later, the officer driving floored it. Mike saw taillights accelerate farther away. To himself, the fresh murderer muttered, "Whew."

He had to go through the populated city of Providence to travel west, where plenty of woods existed. Enough to bury a body.

At 11 p.m., he started digging.

⋆   ⋆   ⋆

Thursday morning at the shop, in the bathroom, Mike unbuttoned his shirt. In the mirror, the bandage seemed to be intact. A dry sanguineous spot on the gauze pad reminded him of the hellish night.

After burying the deceased, he sought out his friend, Dr. Mario; not a medical doctor, but a dentist. Dr. Mario sutured him up good and tight. Mike, a chess player, weighed his moves. The best? Face Frankie Carz man-to-man.

Mike had Frankie's ledgers sitting pretty at the shop's door, like something clever buried in a minefield. The hatless gangster, decked in a dark suit, happened to be right on schedule. "Whatchu do last night, Mikey?"

They squared off, facing each other in the store. "I intend to talk to Don Lorenzo," stated Mike coldly. "The girl was trying to ice me."

"Serves no purpose, involvin' him, Mikey. This quarrel is between us," Frankie edged closer.

Tunneling inside his apron, the artisan whipped out the pistol Veronica had intended to kill him with the previous night. Mike knew perfectly well that the firearm belonged to Frankie—the man bearing such an odious personality, the nemesis he utterly despised. Mike aimed it at the racketeer's breastbone and commanded, "Snatch your books and keep your ass outta here."

Unaccustomed to seeing Mike exhibit such courage, Frankie's hideous façade broadcast a smirk. "You can't get rid of me that easy, Mikey."

Suddenly, they both perceived noise outside. A group of college students appeared about to enter. Mike tucked the .45 back into the apron's pocket. As he was leaving, Frankie sarcastically sanctioned, "Stow the gat, Mikey. Like the dame, I've got another."

That night, Mike revisited the forest and dug again. He did not need the femme fatale's shell, but something close to it. An hour later, he parked two blocks south of the clandestine social club. Using a coat hanger featuring a makeshift loop, he fished until he had the ability to disengage the passenger door lock of Frankie's Cadillac. Mike stuffed Veronica's soiled black dress, scarf, shoes, and hat below the front seat. In the back seat, he ditched the shovel.

He drove for five minutes, spotted a phone booth, inserted a nickel, and put a handkerchief over the mouthpiece.

He heard "State police."

Mike's disguised voice came across muffled. "I have an urgent message for Colonel Hagen. It involves the location of a body buried in the Scituate woods and who dumped it there."

Friday morning, Mike read a *Providence Journal* headline: *Frankie Carlino Arrested on Suspicion of Murder.* Mike sighed, content—for the moment. He figured it seemed reasonable to take his children on a trip for a few days.

*   *   *

Mr. Cappabianca returned from his three-day weekend trip with his daughters, dragging home a suitcase of insuperable problems. These problems weighed down his shoulders like an entire shelf of encyclopedias. He had no idea what the next move in this wicked game had in store for him, but at least the girls would cherish the vacation memories.

Mike did know that Frankie now resided in jail, but that did not necessarily mean he was safe. Beneath his door lay a note written in Italian. It made him nervous.

> *Michele,*
>
>   *Please don't be upset, but the organization has decided to trust someone else with the books. I understand you require days off now and then. I apologize for any financial inconvenience this may cause.*
>
>   *P.S. I had lunch in your father's company*

*yesterday. If you need anything, feel free to come
by the office.*

Holy shit, Mike happily thought. *Too good to be true.
Never going near that office!* He contemplated further,
realizing Ole Shark Face couldn't have talked. But
still, the Frankie issue remained on the table.

His relief was short-lived when Colonel Hagen's
big black boots came marching inside the shop. The
father of three's heart pounded just as hard. *The jerk
babbled to the cops instead*, Mike uneasily reckoned.

"Where you been, pal?" The colonel's tone was
authoritative.

"Lake George, New York. Took the kids."

"Does the name Frankie Carlino mean anything
to you?"

During the five-second pause, the question sent
sweat oozing from the pores on Mike's neck, just
below his posterior hairline, like when a drunken
cowboy unloads a cylinder of .38 shells into a Texas
oil drum. There existed a secret to confess, but Mike
reckoned the colonel undoubtedly wouldn't raise his
offspring as he rotted in a cell behind rolled iron.

"Maybe by way of the newspapers," Mike lied.

"Hmm. Figured all you Eyetalians knew each
other."

"Not really."

"Well, over the weekend, they discovered him
shanked in his prison cell. His death is going to make

today's papers." The colonel removed his large hat and playfully spun it on a long finger. "I guess certain inmates didn't appreciate him strangling the woman he buried up in Scituate. She had reported him to the local police a month prior for giving her a fat lip. Bad feller."

Mike felt as if he had just won a jackpot. *It was a bad dream*, the painter thought to himself.

Before he could utter an audible word, Colonel Hagen said, "Now, about those signs."

The door to his dirty little secret slammed shut— never to be reopened. Mike smiled. "Yes, how can I help you, Colonel Hagen?"

3

LAST DAY

It was a warm, sticky, September day in Camden, New Jersey, 1947. A Gothic limestone belltower dominated the immediate skyline. Its four spires seemed to touch the heavens, mirroring fingers desperate for redemption. Beyond that, across the Delaware River, downtown Philadelphia sprawled in a haphazard mess, its crammed buildings resembling lumps of ashen clay in a smog monster's hands.

Inside the cavernous cathedral, shadows from flickering votive candles danced on stone walls. In the bleak confines of a confession booth, a man knelt stiffly, the burden of recent sins squeezing his soul like a sponge. The confessional grille slid open accompanied by a sudden hiss. Through the distorted screen, the penitent caught a grainy version of a frowsy-faced, white-haired priest.

"Bless me, Father, for I have sinned," the rough

fellow, owning a pockmarked kisser, disclosed solemnly. "It has been two years since my last confession." The offender's pitch was deep, but it quivered with remorse.

"May the Lord exist in your heart."

"Father, I murdered two men in Philly, undeserving of murder. I'm on the run."

Fifteen seconds of silence followed.

"For your penance," the priest replied firmly, "recite seven Hail Marys, seven Our Fathers, and beg the Lord for forgiveness, my son." He then instructed, displaying a visage of seriousness, "You must turn yourself in to the authorities."

"Yes, Father," acquiesced the black-suit-wearing wrongdoer named Baxter, nodding in accord.

Baxter, all thirty-eight hard years of him, shoulders heavy with guilt, unstuck himself from the bench, slid the curtain aside, and crept toward an unoccupied pew.

The air was thick, carrying incense and contrition, an appropriate stage for the first act of his atonement. Ten minutes later, he constructed a sign of the cross, a gesture more habit than conviction. Next, he donned a dark fedora and tilted it down over a mop of black hair streaked by a smidge of gray. Just enough gray to know a thing or two about the earth's cruel ways.

His feet knew the path to the police station, but Baxter wasn't in the business of traveling straight lines. He had a few stops to make, loose threads to tie, and sins to square before the day brought in darkness.

★   ★   ★

Two blocks west, on a façade, Baxter saw an orange-and-blue Rexall sign advertising "PARKER'S DRUGS." Inside, young adults sipping milkshakes filled the counter. Some stared. Flaunting an unappealing phiz atop his six-foot-one frame, which limped during ambulation, he had become used to the gawks. The limp was courtesy of a thug who had taken out his kneecap in 1940.

Walking by, the fugitive heard someone yell, "Are they finally planning to fire Connie Mack this year?" Baxter continued toward the establishment's rear and squeezed his wide torso inside the middle phone booth. The sinner's powerful, slab-like hand, veins protruding, picked up a receiver. Seven digits were dialed.

Baxter sighed. "Betty."

He listened.

"Our job got gaffed up. I iced two guards," he divulged gravely.

He listened and noticed a message engraved in the wood stating, *Call Susan for a thrill*. His lips curled.

"You remember," he asked, "that old abandoned farmhouse in Chester where we hid Grease Spot Sal?"

He listened and chipped at the veneer, using a dirty fingernail.

"Yep...Pennsylvania," he acknowledged smoothly, still chipping. "Wait a month; there's probably going to be a tail on your ass. The loot's all yours."

Baxter spied through the booth's window at the soda counter patrons, enjoying an existence he realized he'd never experience again. It caused him to purse his pallid, chapped lips. Again, he listened.

"No, I need to pay for my mistake. I visited a priest."

He squinted his hazel eyes and listened once more, but now only catching fragments. Baxter then terminated the conversation, saying, "See you in another life, Gorgeous."

*   *   *

Baxter egressed Parker's Pharmacy. He lumbered along, reflecting upon his childhood. His mind sketched an image of a five-year-old boy weeping as his father, a stern man of English descent, packed a measly suitcase and walked out of their derelict three-room flat, leaving it devoid of words. He never saw his dad again; now, all he carried was the man's name.

His next vision was of a young Italian mother living in a world deeply unfamiliar to her. She attempted to discipline him as her absent husband had but failed. By the time John Baxter was ten years old, the wooden spoons his mamma struck him with were breaking in half.

He had not been to the apartment building in two years. It appeared as neglected as ever. On the third floor, he thumped on a door. A short, stout, gray-haired woman answered, garbed in a threadbare cotton dress. Odors of Sicily traveled up his olfactory nerve.

"Johnny," she asked in broken English, "what-uh did you-uh do-uh?" She flailed two beefy extremities in the air. "It's uh all ovuh the radio. You-uh rob bank. Killa two-uh people."

"I'm sorry, Momma," he uttered earnestly, gripping his broad chin. "The guards weren't supposed to die."

"Leta me...fix you-uh meal."

"No, Momma. Not now." She cowered into his arms.

Baxter hugged his mother and slightly pushed her backward, as if it were their last dance. The instant her rotund hind banged the tiny pine kitchen table, he removed one hand from her soft flesh. He fished within a suit pocket and, unbeknownst to her, dropped two wads of cash on the table.

The man gone wrong broke her clutch. Mrs. Baxter's prominent eyes wept—torrents spilling from a broken dam.

Knowing he had to leave, the son suppressed his own tears. "Goodbye, Momma."

★   ★   ★

Back on the sidewalk, Baxter's gaze shifted to a modest jewelry store and spotted an older, petite gent modeling a walrus mustache, fiddling with the front door's lock. Suddenly, a weathered-looking man brushed against the jeweler's keister. The uncanny stranger, wearing a green windbreaker, offered a brief hand gesture in apology, then vamoosed, slipping into the shadows of the closest alley.

Baxter, exhibiting a disturbed countenance, trailed what was perceived as a pickpocket. In the desolate alley, Weather Face extracted the stolen wallet and began counting cash. Baxter dawdled by, gazing away, uninterested. Catching the unknown by surprise, he deftly applied a right-handed, iron claw of a grip to the hood's neck.

The gaunt thief formed a fist which would not have hurt a hemophiliac. He immediately unclenched it, grew wide-eyed, counter-aggression halted.

"Aren't you—?" he spat out in awe.

"Yep it's me," Baxter retorted, administering a series of violent left backhands, maintaining a tenacious grip. "And I rob banks, not ordinary citizens."

The antithesis went unchallenged as ole Weather Face's heinie slid down the cement wall, resembling a toboggan on ice. Standing over his opponent, Baxter grimaced as though he had recently gurgled apple cider vinegar.

The ironic good-doer returned to the now-ready-for-business jewelry store. The elder asked, "Can I assist you?"

Baxter plopped one wallet on the display case. "Lose something?" he exhaled, recovering his breath.

The pint-sized merchant checked his pockets. "Wait! That man," the jeweler reckoned logically, "the one who bumped into me?"

"Yep."

* * *

A block east, Baxter observed a feeble, elderly lady sporting an outdated cloche hat. The woman was attempting to climb four concrete outdoor stairs, lugging two grocery bags, a wooden cane wedged between them.

He stepped forward, his palm supine, the rough edges softened as he formed the gesture. "Ma'am, let me help."

"Thank you," she agreed, gratefully. "Second floor."

He took the load, and she opened the door of an apartment complex. The place was no better than where his mom lived. Childhood memories briefly resurfaced as the spinster laboriously ascended the stairs. Tailing behind, Baxter wondered how she would ever have made it if not for his assistance.

As he proceeded up from the ground-floor apartment below to the right, he detected muffled voices which sounded like absolute chaos. They ebbed as he scaled higher. At the top, once she became settled, he passed the bags to her one at a time. Her gaudy perfume compelled him to hold his breath, similar to when someone expels unwanted air from their buttocks during an elevator ride.

Appreciating Baxter's ministration, she remarked, "Sonny, they don't make fellers of your kind anymore."

He chuckled. "Well...."

Baxter descended the fissured stairs but stopped to sit on the third step. He pretended to tie his shoe but was more interested in the turmoil beyond the door of apartment number one. Just his luck that its door gaped.

"Where are you goin', Ernie?" bleated a female voice bitterly.

A threshold separated an attractive, mid-twenties blonde and a tall, gawky man in a brown suit. Somewhere distal to the blonde, an infant possessing healthy lungs cried as if its bottle had run dry.

"Shut up!" snarled the unfamiliar man. Towering over the stressed female, the bully called Ernie delivered a vicious slap against her painted-up face.

"Bastard!" she countered hysterically, holding her left cheek.

"Goin' to a bar. You'd ought to be here when I git home," growled the abuser, "and fix my suppa."

The abused slammed the door shut.

To Baxter, the inarticulate Ernie growled, "Whaddaya lookin' at, pally?"

Baxter shrugged big shoulders. "The frail's not my problem." Johnny Baxter comprehended he could lick the bully, but something better came to mind. Ernie's departure left behind a gloomy chill in the hallway. Baxter knew the police station was temporarily on hold. He figured he should go see Fatso anyway.

⋆ ⋆ ⋆

He walked until an unlit neon sign advertising *Camden Bowling Lanes* hung above his head. Baxter shoved one of the glass double doors.

The bowling alley was so desolate that the Dormouse would have unearthed Wonderland in any corner. He approached a counter and nodded to an attendant who might be best described as mirroring Ben Franklin, including the spectacles.

The colonial-looking relic cracked the ice first. "Baxsta." The drawl was sluggish.

"Schultz." Baxter peered at the clerk, employing serious eyes.

"Wut?"

"Where's Fatso?"

"Where's yuh think?" the attendant, known as Schultz, quipped sardonically.

Baxter pitched a guess. "The office."

Baxter menacingly strutted to the rear of the establishment. He passed a door reading *Gentleman's Lounge.* He glanced behind, making sure he was clear of Schultz's sight, slid open a wall display case, and pulled out a large bowling trophy.

He kicked wide another door—*Private*—then plodded along a dingy hallway. To his left, a fat man

sporting three chins sat at a desk in a cluttered office, a cloud of cigar smoke eddying north of his head. Baxter's fierce mug loomed in the doorway, unsmiling.

"I presumed you'd be on the lam," the corpulent entrepreneur frankly stated in a frothy, asthmatic voice.

"You fucked me, Fatso."

"Huh?" Fatso puffed his torpedo.

"Those three bushers you sent me," Baxter imparted angrily, "caused me to shoot those two guards. Your henchmen couldn't even tie rope."

Fatso shrugged, a slow, malevolent grin spreading upon his face. "Not my fault."

"Was hoping you'd say that, Fatso."

Grasping it by the upper brass figurine, he unveiled the bulky trophy from his posterior side, reached across the desk, and clocked the fat businessman two inches above his eyebrows with its marble base. Fatso's cranium careened, not sure which way to land. Before it could decide, Baxter hammered a full series of frontal lobe trophy strikes. Fatso's blood splattered all over Baxter and any other object which would accept it.

The sitting dead man's body was now slumped rearwards. Baxter milled his victim's cigar and placed the sanguineous makeshift weapon on the desk adjacent to the corpse. The murderer wanted him found in such fashion.

Baxter returned to the public area, relieved himself in the lounge, and scrubbed his two stained hands.

On his path back to Schultz, he stood facing a row of cubical lockers stacked four high. He groped into one pocket for a key and opened unit number 101—his locker.

As he expected, his spare Colt and a duffel bag were there. The locker portion of the bowling alley stop was not planned, but a guy he encountered named Ernie had changed all that.

Schultz, behind the register, knowing what kinds of things Fatso's associates kept in certain lockers, shrewdly took notice. "Dat time, eh?"

Baxter, passing by, did not really fathom what the jargon meant but replied, "Yep." But one thing Baxter felt sure about was indolent Schultz had to be unaware of Fatso's execution.

The Ben Franklin clone spat in a garbage can.

"Oh yeah, Schultz," Baxter mocked sarcastically, turning his head, "I understand they're giving out speaking lessons for a song down the street."

"Shud up, Baxsta."

"Go check on your boss," Baxter advised drily. "Bet he wants to see you in his chambers. Needs a shoe shine." Baxter cackled as he propelled through the double doors, smelling fresh air.

*   *   *

Baxter was familiar with the compact savings and loan institution, but even more accustomed to when they would unbolt its safe. The timing seemed perfect, although small jobs were not his usual. The joint stood off the main drag, and a lack of lighting made it analogous to King Tut's tomb.

Thirty seconds after entering, a middle-aged security guard, clothed in a brown uniform, felt cold metal press deep into his latissimus dorsi muscle.

"Baxter," the man brandishing the tin badge scoffed, holding up two thin extremities, "everyone knows you here."

The watchman's dissuasion fell on deaf ears. "Sorry, Charlie...nothing personal."

Baxter delivered a judo chop to Charlie's dorsal neck. The gent toppled, similar to a sack of potatoes being booted off a farm truck.

"Keep low, Charlie," the bank robber directed, confiscating the wimp's firearm. "Grasp the fact I got two under my belt this week."

Utilizing the borrowed heater, the three other workers and one customer were herded like cattle towards the open safe. Baxter, calm as a windless tunnel, stuffed the guard's gun into his pocket, then simultaneously pointed his own Colt at a portly, half-bald manager in a gray suit that screamed "buy one, get one." Subsequently, he motioned the firearm at some canvas satchels hanging inside the vault.

To the manager, he barked, "Fill up two. Big bills!" Half Baldy responded to the requisition with alacrity, moving as if his existence depended on it.

When the moolah exchanged hands, Baxter squeezed the bulging sacks into his own battered duffel.

Baxter spoke his parting words to the folks in the unlocked vault: "Stay on your bellies for ten minutes, or from jail, I'll arrange for someone to cut up your families into jigsaw puzzle pieces." The fib put a simper, crooked as his trade, on Baxter's coarse facade.

Outside, Baxter treaded to an intersection, pulled on a cab door, and ordered, "Don't touch the meter." He propped a C-note in front of an oily-faced cabby's nostrils.

The man understood this to be two weeks' wages. "Gotcha."

Baxter uttered only one sentence to the hack operator: "Corner of Broadway and Pine."

*   *   *

Baxter scurried through a string of deserted alleys, his urgent footsteps echoing against the damp walls. Prior to entering the dwelling, he discarded the guard's piece in a sewer hole. He thumped on the apartment door using his big three knuckles.

The comely blonde-headed woman from an hour ago popped the door ajar, showing a puzzled countenance. She wore a flowered housecoat; the heister could not tell what else. Baxter no longer heard the baby crying as he unzipped the duffel bag enough for her to see greenbacks.

"Take it," he said, dropping the load at her bare feet, "and board the first train to Arlington, Virginia."

She peered down at the bag. "Mr.—"

"There's an address inside. My friend's wife in Virginia will help you."

She stalled, gathering her thoughts like scattered pieces. "But—"

"Get packin' now," he urged. "You don't want this slug fathering that baby." He gestured one finger outside, then rotated it back toward her apartment as he said it.

She focused on him, not drawn to his looks, but to the raw masculinity he exuded. Soon, she gawked low at the bag once more, mimicking a bear hunting for salmon.

"Put it all in one suitcase," he advised.

"Thank you," she sobbed, "for a new life."

*   *   *

Today's sky remained powder blue, like those three cheap properties in Monopoly. Baxter resumed his trek to the police station. He figured he might get lucky and the boys in blue might pick him up on today's job, offering a ride.

On the sidewalk, alongside a horse-drawn open-air pushcart, he beheld a yellow ball of feathers hobbling about. Knowing it was not a street survivor such as himself, he waved both arms, snagging the attention of a nearby vegetable vendor.

Baxter pointed at the canary. "Yours?"

The hawker, showcasing a bristly mug above puny shoulders, shook his dome impassively.

This bird won't survive out here, the bank robber internally reflected.

Baxter grabbed a wooden crate off the ground; the vendor offered no objection. The plumed creature was secured. He limped, hauling the box to the nearest complex, then rapped on a door. As he waited, his brain talked, *Will I ever get to the precinct?*

An oversized, oblong-skulled man in flannel pajamas appeared.

Baxter probed, "You lose a canary?"

"Next door. Apartment two," the grump growled. His chunky index finger showed the way.

Baxter disdainfully gazed at the pajamas. Under his breath, he muttered, "It's past noon."

He rapped on the succeeding door. A college-age girl, dressed akin to a jock, answered hastily and saw her bird in the crate.

"How can I repay, sir?" Her raspy tone was full of gratitude.

"Take better care of him," Baxter instructed curtly, handing her the pet.

"It's a she."

Baxter shrugged, did a one-hundred-eighty-degree turn, descended the steps, and was gone like Fatty Arbuckle movies.

⋆　⋆　⋆

Baxter's excursion continued. He became enticed by an A&P Supermarket sign. *Let me fetch one last Coke,* he thought. The market appeared uncrowded, and Baxter was quite familiar with the location of the soda cooler.

As he approached the cashiers, he stopped in his tracks. His astute eyes noticed a hefty cashier transferring a bill from the register to her blouse pocket between transactions.

He strode to the service desk. "Hey, George," Baxter relayed tersely, "number three is pilfering."

"Excuse me?" responded a buck-toothed, red-headed man owning a skeleton frame.

"You heard me."

"Baxter, you know I have to phone the police." His tone aired cynical.

"Might be tough to prove," Baxter countered, casting a persuasive stare. "Simply fire her."

"On you."

"I see. Didn't figure you as a reader of newspapers. Well...that'll save me some steps."

"Eh?"

Fatso's executioner sauntered to the Coke cooler, popped the cap thanks to the assistance of a metal shelf, and chugged. Understanding that his freedom was limited, he savored the moment. *They can't arrest me twice,* he reckoned internally, glancing at his watch and realizing he had about seven minutes of amusement remaining.

Expelling a grunt, Baxter reached for a pouch of potato chips and split the seal, echoing a man tearing apart a bad memory. He then started eating handfuls, chuckling to what was perceived as an audience of none.

A freckle-faced lad five years out of diapers poked his head around the corner, awestruck and innocent, completely unaware of the legend of Johnny Baxter.

The youth spoke first. "Cool, mista: eat now, pay later."

Baxter smirked, raising one finger to his lips in an impish shush gesture. "Or don't pay at all."

"Hey, mista," the youth pleaded, "wanna play cops 'n' robbers?"

Baxter transformed his meaty hand into an imaginary pistol. "Sure...I'll be the robber."

The youth aimed and clicked a Roy Rogers die-cast pistol. Baxter held four fingers over his abdomen. "You got me. Okay, scram, kid—lemme enjoy my final meal in peace."

Sirens blasted in the background through the store's closed windows. Baxter realized he was past the point of no return. His humor turned to nervousness. For the first time today, he began to sweat.

Unexpectedly, the kid doubled back to the aisle's corner, peeping as if he'd caught his parents doing something naughty. When man and boy established eye contact, the lad withdrew.

"Wait, kid!" Baxter hollered.

The spying orb reappeared.

"Be anything in life besides a criminal." Baxter knew the following minute would linger in the lad's perspective forever.

Pounding footsteps and commotion erupted through the grocery establishment as the scattered few still browsing froze, their eyes darting. Baxter got on his knees, fished for the Colt, then tossed it onto the cold, cracked tiles. He placed both upper limbs skyward, surrendering to fate.

Six men in blue swarmed the aisle like flies on a corpse. One yelled sanctimoniously, "Freeze, Baxter," his voice tight, radiating enough righteousness to wear a halo.

From the stunned onlookers' perspective, the whole scenario looked rehearsed.

To the peeping child, Baxter barked emphatically, "See?"

★   ★   ★

At the Camden train station platform, a woman carried a suitcase in one hand and her infant in the other. She tried hard to maintain normal respirations.

The porter asked, "Can I take the baggage, ma'am?"

She gripped the handle resolutely. "No, it stays with me."

4

THE MAN NEXT DOOR

It was a sharp September afternoon in '47, a type of day when the sun hits the flawed sidewalks so perfectly, it makes you forget the undesirables crawling around town. In a hardscrabble Chillicothe, Ohio, neighborhood, where telephone poles stood like sentinels, a geriatric, hatless man perched himself on the sagging porch of a rundown, single-floor dwelling. The house, the color of faded straw, sat surrounded by grass that hadn't met a mower in weeks, an unruly contrast against the trimmed lawns of adjacent properties. Behind it all, one smokestack from the Mead Paper Company loomed large, like a queen piece casting its shadow over a pawn-filled chessboard.

The man was a ghost of his former self, residing in a home of forgotten dreams. His wild, unkempt white hair looked like it hadn't seen a comb in months, with a dome as bald as a billiard ball on top, not having sprouted a hair since the Woodrow Wilson administration. The gentleman's eyes burned, showcasing a jaundiced glow from his skull like headlights on a foggy night. He wore a rumpled white shirt that had seen better days, gray trousers that didn't quite sit right, and no tie to speak of. Nobody seemed to recall his real name. To Mrs. Anderson, the neighborhood busybody one door over, he was simply "The Man Next Door."

Eighty feet away, inside of a modest two-story cottage, Mrs. Anderson stood at a sink, washing dishes in a flowered dress that clung to her like a cheap alibi. Her love handles spilled laterally from either side, resembling two inquisitive turtle heads poking out of their shells. She was in her mid-thirties, stout, carrying a round face that had known too many disappointments, but her eyes—they were emerald green, knifelike, calculating. The woman paused for a beat, her soapy hands suspended in the air. Through the window, she watched her five-year-old daughter tumbling about in a lower-middle-class yard that appeared abandoned by folks brave enough to climb the corporate ladder.

Young Ruth Anderson danced among the flowers. Locks of golden hair bounced with each sway, exuding innocence.

The Man Next Door, who usually sat his hind towards the Anderson property, rose slowly from a rickety green metal chair, descended the crumbling steps,

and dawdled to his outdated 1932 flat-roof Plymouth. Two scuffed black shoes dragged on cracked cement during each progression, like a rustle of swept leaves. Before slipping into the driver's seat, he paused, peering narrowly over shrubs, as though searching for something—or someone—just out of reach.

To young Ruth, he said, "Hi, little girl, what's your name?" The man's voice sounded croaky, but his tone aired benign.

"Not going to tell you anymore, mister," she replied cutely. "You always forget." Her rosy cheeks got brighter.

Unable to hear any of the dialogue, Mrs. Anderson vigilantly eyeballed them from her post just beyond the panes of a half-opened window, steady as a lighthouse scanning the reef for hidden wrecks. She was not nervous. The man exhibited himself as feeble enough that he had to be harmless.

Once started, the vintage car crept out of its driveway and went right at a corner just past the Anderson cottage.

Ruth's early teenage brother, Teddy Anderson, and his friends were wrestling on the other edge of the yard, distal to her. Teddy was a burly lad, much bigger than his peers. All five boys quit tussling, reached for the grass, and then tossed chestnuts at the auto as it cruised past.

Ding, ding, ding was registered by all, including the occupant. The vehicle stopped. The four subordinates hid behind Teddy, who stood erect. The egressing elder pointed an emphatic, crooked finger over his Plymouth's square roof.

"Whatcha gonna do about it, Grandpa?" the bully growled, folding his arms with a sneer.

The partially hidden pranksters hooted from Teddy's rear as if they were being amused by Fibber McGee on the radio. Disgusted, the aged fellow drove off.

★   ★   ★

Ninety minutes later, the senior citizen returned in a heap chock-full of goods. Ted's coterie was now seated on a stone wall, watching the man incompetently navigate into his driveway.

"What's he do with all that stuff?" a freckle-faced boy named Charlie asked inquisitively. Charlie served as the one kid in the neighborhood whose nose always dripped like a faucet.

"Theodore!" barked Mrs. Anderson, louder than necessary. "Come in. Supper!" The party broke up.

The second-largest boy in Teddy's crew, Homer, trotted by the dilapidated hovel.

The Man Next Door solicited, "Hey, youngster, give me a hand."

"I need to get home for dinner," the adolescent countered tersely.

"Take just a second," the seeker implored, beckoning arthritically bent fingers. For the youth, curiosity caused him to follow those fingers.

Brown-haired Homer, a baseball cap pulled low over his brow, grunted as he hoisted his half of the cardboard box, storing a dozen or more heavy cast-iron pans. The kid couldn't make sense of it, couldn't understand why anyone would need that many pans.

Once they were inside, the stranger slammed the door shut by employing a swift kick, causing splinters of peeling wood to fly as if the house was sneezing.

The residence had a somber aura, similar to a graveyard at twilight. Darkness lurked in each corner. A putrid smell, thick and sour, assailed Homer's nasal cavity, sticking to the back of his throat. The atmosphere felt dense, weighed down by something unseen, the walls themselves waiting anxiously.

The minor's not fully grown body filled with a sense of trepidation as a shiver slid down his vertebral column—the pit of his stomach twisting. Instinct told him to drop the box and run; however, his feet acted as though they were jammed in quicksand.

The man jerked a bony chin toward one room, his silent command hanging in the sullen air. It was meant to be a bedroom, but it might as well have been a tomb. Neither could ingress further than a foot.

Pots and pans piled in cardboard cartons were layered high enough to resemble a makeshift stockade. Bewildered, Homer stood frozen, caught in the uncanny scene. The former haven for sleep had turned into a warehouse of lifeless goods, boxes on boxes crammed into every inch of the place. One bed was nothing but a mountain of stacked debris, the top of it scraping the ceiling like a dead man's last breath.

Where does this man sleep? the juvenile wondered.

In a hallway alcove, Homer spotted a case containing a war medal, its yellow ribbon trimmed with two slender blue stripes near the edges. Above it hung a weathered cap featuring an insignia of crossed rifles. Somehow, it abated his fears.

"Civil War?" questioned the stripling.

"No, son, not possible. Spanish American." The man's affect presented as flat.

"Oh."

Homer's wandering eyes noticed a modest wooden chest atop a tabouret. The senile man encroached upon the youth's space and pressed his palm against the top of it.

"Do not open," he directed impassionedly.

"What's inside?"

"Protection."

Homer continued the perusal, employing a cat burglar's caution; his steps feathered across the floor. Soon, both eyes bulged, then his mouth gaped. On a cluttered kitchen table lay a kitchen knife. Its handle had been grotesquely mummified with what looked like an entire roll of electrical tape. The tape created a large, inordinate handle fit for a gorilla. Homer shuffled back three paces, his breath faltering, a retreat as deliberate as a gambler folding a bad hand.

The Man Next Door attempted to intervene. "Hey, that's—"

Homer caught just enough to set his nerves tingling before bolting towards the miniscule foyer. The war veteran followed, but the schoolboy opened the door, stepped beyond its threshold, and vanished. Outside, the hoarder's weary eyes traced the outline of a panicked kid racing up the incline, swallowed by the dense shadows of the apple trees.

Once Homer felt safe and breathless, he knew he couldn't wait to tell his cohorts what he had discovered. Being the kid delivering such a scoop would surely bring him glory tomorrow.

Ten minutes later, a burly motorcycle cop rumbled onto the scene, his steely gaze locking on the jalopy parked at a crooked slant. He killed the bike's engine, eased his helmet onto the seat, and stopped below the porch stairs.

His voice, calm but laced with assertiveness, broke the heavy air. "Seems to me this heap's sporting a few new dents since last week. Been wondering if it's on the block. My boy could use a set of wheels, money's tight." His thick, greasy paws groped the uneven contours of the rusty metal, glancing up at the porch between touches. "Jeez...vandals, was it?"

"No, some foreigner hit me on the road," the elder explained unemotionally. "They couldn't even speak English."

The cop scratched his head.

The packrat continued, "You should be trying to find out who keeps breaking into my place."

"Eh?"

"I made a bologna sandwich," the Man Next Door divulged, "put it on a plate, covered it, took a nap, and when I awoke, I learned someone ate it."

"Do you have any children in town I may contact?"

"No. Why?"

The lawman's lumpy face appeared concerned.

Meanwhile, the assiduous Mrs. Anderson gazed through one kitchen window. Her husband, a skinny, blonde-headed man dressed in an olive suit and owner of a face that looked like someone had just dunked it in burnt porridge, listened.

"A policeman is speaking alongside our neighbor," the wife said, pausing as her eyes narrowed at the thought. "We've been here three months, and we don't even know his name"

"He's not very friendly," Mr. Anderson acknowledged uninterestedly, picking up a fork. "It's why nobody knows his name."

"Ruth might."

"Pardon?" He glanced up, as if the statement had thrown him off guard.

"She talks to him."

"Where is Ruth?"

"Playing upstairs."

"Alright."

"Maybe we ought to invite him over for supper

one night," she suggested, toying with the edge of her apron, a faint smile creeping across her face.

Mr. Anderson signaled apathy by raising both margins of a newspaper and plunging his head into the sports page.

★   ★   ★

A day passed. Late morning light projected through the blinds, casting stripes on the Man Next Door as he trudged to the fridge, still wearing yesterday's tousled getup. By means of a quick jerk, he pulled out something wrapped in greasy brown paper—his expression unreadable. He drifted toward a closet, the kind of place that hid secrets. Reaching up, he raised a pile of dusty magazines off the high shelf, slid the cold, mysterious bundle beneath it, and closed the door with a finality that echoed loud enough to make a ghoul jump.

The oldster added a stained khaki-colored windbreaker to his repeated attire, then journeyed into town via automobile, stopping at a small department store. Once indoors, he casually put various merchandise on a counter. A twentyish store clerk, possessing a puny torso and oversized black glasses, focused keenly on the pile his customer had erected.

"Back again, sir," the young fellow remarked tartly. "All sale items, I see."

"Please ring me up. I have to get going. I had to hide my lunchmeat in the closet."

"Huh?" The clerk seemed confused; squiggly lines creased his forehead.

"They break into my house," the elder imparted, "and steal my food if I'm not home."

"Why don't you lock your doors?" the sales associate asked flippantly, rolling his eyes slightly, the gesture almost imperceptible.

"Won't help. They built some kind of contraption which goes under the front door, then unlocks it by way of the interior side."

"Unusual." The counter helper's cadence conveyed disbelief in what he had just heard. He packed the smaller wares inside a cardboard box. "Who are these people?" he prodded halfheartedly just to play along, finding humor in the man's delusions.

"I never see them. These intruders mostly invade at night to poke around," the Man Next Door revealed. "By the time I wake up, they are gone." The clerk helped load the goods into the clunker and was happy when the individual showcasing such an odd demeanor drove yonder.

*   *   *

Thirty minutes afterward, the man resettled home, pulling into his driveway. He transferred the boxes into the shanty, then positioned himself in a desultory fashion in his ordinary spot.

The same motorcycle policeman from yesterday revisited and dismounted. The patrolman made a mental note of a newly acquired huge dent on the right front fender and a shattered headlight.

"Sir, I'm back, responding to an accident," the copper said sharply. "A hit-and-run." He protruded his chest as if it were loaded with helium.

"She hit me. Didn't speak English. A Mexican."

The copper's timbre changed to authoritative. "Sir, it was a male. A city official. American."

"Oh."

"Going to give you a citation and have this jalopy impounded."

A while later, Mrs. Anderson spied through the window. Her green eyes widened as the old-timer's archaic wreck was hauled off by a rusted truck bearing the faded lettering: *Harold's Garage*. It presented as a kind of spectacle that bred suspicion.

★   ★   ★

At 5 p.m., the sky turned battleship gray. The Man Next Door perched alone in the usual spot, detached from his surroundings, indifferent to his dire situation. Ruth frolicked in the yard. Mrs. Anderson saw Teddy's bunch close to her. Satisfied, she went downstairs to the basement, hauling a laundry basket.

Homer stood in the middle of the cluster of boys, orally exaggerating his experience within the geezer's residence one day prior. When the story grew tired and Homer was out of yarns, Teddy and his crew of juveniles stepped onto the walkway. They moseyed past the driveway where a car had been towed an hour prior. Charlie synthesized his voice to simulate Donald Duck, then discourteously taunted, "Hey, Father Time."

The other rascals guffawed. The smallest boy, Gary, stretched a diminutive arm up in the air, pretended to be pulling down a make-believe rope, then farted. Additional laughter erupted. The unsmiling elder observed them marching up the hill until they looked analogous to a group of army ants.

Ruth now played in solitude. On the adjacent road, a black sedan descended its steep hill. As the hardtop reached the Anderson cottage, it tapered and braked hard. Its occupant hurriedly leaped out.

At the driveway's periphery, a scrawny male owning black, vacant eyes, dressed in a galaxy blue suit, ogled the child.

The Man Next Door caught the sharp cry of the young girl's protest, her words slicing through motionless air: "You're not my daddy!" Subsequently, a blood-curdling shriek pierced through his ear canal like a serpent.

The relic hastily rose and entered his mangy house, leaving the door ajar. In the Anderson driveway, the thin, malevolent man was dragging Ruth by her bare foot. The posterior aspect of the victim's head and elbows was scraping the unforgiving driveway's pavement, causing her throat to expel a symphony of pain-filled screams.

The abductor had progressed to the sidewalk when the candescent-eyed veteran faced him and aimed a firearm.

Next, the elder's revolver roared three times, blasting three slugs into the predator's cranium. The bastard, still holding tight to Ruth's ankle like a leech, crumpled to the pavement. The attack on Ruth became thwarted.

The senior shooter watched Ruth as she executed a rapid twist of her ankle, easily breaking the dead man's grasp and sprinting towards her house. The Anderson door exploded open. Hearing gunshots and seeing her neighbor nonchalantly egress the scene, after sticking the piece inside his windbreaker's pocket, Mrs. Anderson stood thunderstruck. Her dress billowed in September's wind.

Witnessing a corpse on the sidewalk, the housewife dashed to meet Ruth halfway in their driveway, her meaty legs moving swiftly.

"Mommy...? Mommy, a bad man tried to take me."

She picked up her daughter, both screaming. An odor of propellant pervaded the immediate atmosphere. With her daughter's arms clinging around her abdomen, the mother bolted into the Anderson cottage and dialed the police station.

"A man has been shot on the sidewalk," she shared hysterically, "in front of my home! Thirty-four Birch Street."

Mrs. Anderson listened, then replied, "No, I don't know him."

Sirens blared in the distance. Arriving initially were two uniformed patrolmen who looked akin to stoic, square-faced siblings. The duo swaggered out.

Officer #1 stared at the recumbent, lifeless figure. Officer #2 removed his pistol from its holster and did a three-hundred-sixty-degree turn for surveillance. The area was secure.

Mrs. Anderson's heart thumped, similar to a Tommy gun, as she returned to her yard, lugging a forty-pound, sniffling Ruth. She glimpsed at the dwelling next door and perceived what appeared to be an unfazed person lingering on the porch in his desired spot.

The woman now considered the man—she never put a name to him—a hero, her hero. Mrs. Anderson's fingers trembled when she released Ruth and directed, "Ruth, go in the house."

Using a voice full of resonance, Officer #1 questioned brusquely, "Ma'am, what happened here?"

Before she spoke, the mother, hyperventilating, steeled herself for a final view of what she regarded as a dead monster sprawled on the pavement. A monster that nearly ruined her family, one who died carrying a distorted face, compliments of bullet holes.

The moment she phoned the police station a few minutes prior, Mrs. Anderson just knew she would protect her novel crusader. The shaken witness steadied herself.

"Officers," Mrs. Anderson lied through her teeth, "I saw a big, fat fellow in a white sedan stop his car and shoot the man."

"Ma'am, start from the beginning, go fast," Officer #2 commanded.

"You see, originally, I gazed out my window and noticed a strange automobile parked," she fabricated. "An unfamiliar man was going into its trunk when another vehicle arrived. The first man started running. A second man exited his own vehicle and began shooting. He then took off. It looked like something from the gangster pictures."

"Around here?" Officer #1 responded sneeringly.

"Must be headin' to Cincinnati or Columbus," pitched in Officer #2 sanctimoniously, not doubting the lady's veracity of the narrative.

To his partner, Officer #1 ordered, "Notify the other units."

Officer #2 barreled to his black and white and relayed the message over the radio.

Officer #1 peeked past the shrubs at the lone male on the porch. He walked there and climbed the steps.

"Sir, sir." Using two beefy digits, Officer #1 nudged the white-haired man's right shoulder and bluntly asked, "Did you see the fella that sped away?"

The executioner offered a blank stare, void of emotion. No verbal response.

Officer #1's tone was irate. "Mister, quick. What-cha see?"

The Man Next Door glanced into the police-man's brown eyes—an attempted stall to collect his thoughts—while, on his lap, his hands twisted, work-ing themselves into knots. He replied flatly, "I...I can't remember."

Thirty minutes later, back inside the cramped cot-tage, Mrs. Anderson laid out an extra place setting at the Formica table. Her hands trembled just once; then steadied, moving with a quiet resolve. Tonight, one special guest, one more mouth to feed, and a debt no mother could repay.

5

TWO BIRDS, ONE STONE

New Paris, one of America's largest cities—September, '47. In lower downtown, known by locals as Old Downtown, a black, metal, elongated sign hung stubbornly atop a ninth-floor office door. This modest sign, in the architecturally outdated eleven-story cement Keiser Building, advertised *Max Weatherbee, Private Detective for Hire.*

Ursula paused at the threshold, one low-heeled shoe in the waiting room, the other in Max Weatherbee's sanctum, the hem of a sensible violet dress brushing her calves. Her hair, the color of gutter ash, sat pulled back in a no-nonsense bun. The part-time secretary looked aged enough to collect Social Security, yet too young for the morgue.

"I'm heading out, Max," the elder female imparted, her voice boring like a silent movie marathon. "Seems as if our five o'clock's dragging both feet."

Six-foot-one, thirty-five-year-old Max Weatherbee had a forehead wide and flat as a sheet of steel, resembling something stamped by the Motor Vehicle Bureau. His face bore the rough-hewn appearance of a man who'd endured more than his share of brawls and came out grinning.

Slight creases framed his features, aged not by years but by life's blows, taken plus given. He was clean-shaven—no mustache to allow for distraction—which only sharpened a square, Hollywood tough-guy jaw. The kind that made dames shoot a second gander and caused fellas to wonder if he'd once fought for money. His chin matched the build: sturdy, dimpled, defiant. A full head of shiny coal-colored hair swept neatly from a hard part carved down to the scalp, streaked with enough gray to lend him a touch of gravitas. Today, he presented himself in a blue pinstriped suit and red tie.

Max Weatherbee's lair was spare and methodical, every inch laid out with purpose. A hulking steel desk anchored the room beneath the low hum of a fluorescent fixture that never shut up. The walls wore a coat of drab green, which did nothing to lift the mood.

No trace of immediate family softened the place, just framed milestones and snapshots of past glories. Max hadn't done well with steady relationships—was it his lack of emotional commitment, or lack of funds? Even he couldn't answer.

Beyond him, twin filing cabinets loomed like

sentries beside a six-paned window. A wooden table sagged under the weight of cameras in various states of assembly. A minibar stood nearby, a scotch bottle on top catching the light like a lure. Beside it, a shut white metal door bore a stark black sign: *Photography Dark Room.*

A Lucky Strike dangled limply between his square lips. He reclined in a red oak bendable chair. The PI's tone aired as flatline serious. "Thank you, Ursula. Please leave the doors open."

Twenty-five minutes later, at exactly 5:27 p.m., she breezed into the waiting room via the public hallway, her presence heavily suffocating the stale air. A dame, a little younger in age than him, bleach blonde, her coif wild in a manner which screamed for attention— the wrong kind.

Max darted then lingered in the threshold leading to his workspace. He ran a thumb along his jaw-line, sizing her up, scanning her from crown to toe and figured she hovered ten pounds away from being chubby.

The lass wasn't his type—too brazen, too expensive, too much on display, borderline *meretricious.* The outfit clung to her frame, a scanty number leaving little to the imagination. Low-cut white blouse, tight black skirt that rode up too high. Beneath a pair of taut nylons, her heels clicked on the marble, echoing a ticking clock; each step reminding Max she was late, yet didn't care. She chewed gum, blaring a snap, entitlement in every pop.

"I have an appointment here at five o'clock," she purred, her voice sugary, edged in the fashion of someone who fancied playing boss.

"Yup," Max replied, a lazy curl tugging at his lip, "and it's five thirty."

She didn't bother rendering an apology. Instead, she plunked herself into the chair across from his desk and irately divulged, "My no-good husband's two-timin' me." She fetched a cigarette from a gold case, then stuck it between polished cherry lips. Max's gold lighter lit it for her and he sat. The gussied-up woman crossed her legs and resumed talking. "Saw your ad in one of those freebie newspapers. I gather you're cheaper than the rest."

He reckoned it wasn't a compliment and resented her impertinence. Max's chestnut brown eyes cast a glare as he asked, "What makes you so sure he's entertaining a side dish, Mrs....?" By way of his note-pad, he knew her name; he wanted to hear how she spat it out.

"Fairchild. Margaret Fairchild." She unfastened an alligator purse and yanked out a scrap of lace. "Found these in his car. The skinny minnies sure as hell ain't mine; not in this decade, anyhow."

The aggrieved wife made a move indicating she might toss them at him. The operative held up a palm in objection.

"I see 'em, Mrs. Fairchild. Maybe the guy's simply got exotic...shall we say, tastes?"

"You act like a feller who doesn't want my money."

Max smirked. He suspected she was about to fork over some cash; however, a few pinpricks couldn't hurt.

"He ain't no weirdo pervert," Margaret Fairchild barked gratingly, puffing smoke. "There's been perfume on his suit, strange charges on the bank book. Little things, but they add up."

The P.I. orated, "My current rate is thirty a day, plus expenses, which includes anything I buy—gasoline, a bite to eat, and lubing the lips of stooges if necessary. Sometimes I summon a street associate to provide extra eyes." He eased a Lucky Strike from the pack and tapped it once. "For this type of a job, I'll start tailing him after he leaves work and keep at it all night if need be. I'll require two hundred for a retainer up front. You got that kind of dough?"

She reopened the reptile-hide purse, stuffed the foreign undergarments inside, then dropped eleven twenties into his sight. He counted it out, slow and deliberate, and slid one Andrew Jackson portrait athwart the desk.

Margaret's green eyes surveyed the place scornfully, then she said, "The extra twenty's a tip in advance. Looks like you could stand to use it."

She slid it back, and he slipped it into his shirt pocket, expelling a dry chuckle, realizing she wasn't kidding. For the time being, he let her have the power she seemed to seek.

He guided a pen and a scrap of paper across the blotter. "Write down your address, where he's employed, plus anything else that might help me dig." He pointed at her using his middle finger—merely one of his bad habits, turned downward at least. "And return my pen. It's a ballpoint."

He could have jotted it himself, but he wanted her to do it. She did as told and began to scribble.

"Call my office," Max advised, sparking the cig hanging from his lip, "every day at noon. If there's news to ascertain, you'll hear it. And toss those undies back in his ride. We don't want hubby gettin' wise."

She nodded her head.

The sleuth pushed a business card across the desk. "If you need to reach me after hours, phone the answering service. Include your initials following the message, not your name."

She nodded once more in muted confirmation. He was in control now, a reverse of the coin.

Margaret Fairchild stood. Max's eyes tracked the sway of her walk toward the exit, figuring a glimpse didn't cost him a wooden nickel.

* * *

A day later. The man Max patiently waited for, beneath a cloudy heaven, bore the name Reginald Fairchild. He worked somewhere inside the Old

Colony Savings Bank. Where he worked didn't matter, but where he went next did. The 1941 Ford V-8 coupe housed Max's buttocks in the interim. He'd purchased it secondhand when he arrived home after the war. It served as a valuable transportation tool for his trade.

At ten past five, a man egressed the financial institution constructed in Gothic Revival architecture and, curbside, urgently hailed a cab. The individual fit the description of Mr. Fairchild. Max had memorized it—tall, narrow shoulders, plus a mustached mug.

The man didn't climb in but instead showed the cabbie a sheet of scrap. They conversed for a few seconds. Soon he casually stuffed the note into his suit jacket pocket, then paced briskly to the gleaming new '47 Chrysler New Yorker that Max was babysitting from a slab afar.

What's the hurry, Fairchild? he wondered.

The opulent Chrysler errantly weaved through busy streets, as if the destination were unfamiliar. Max covertly trailed several automobile lengths back.

The thoroughfares blurred into sameness, spilling onto a city block with a half-dozen identical, wizened, five-story tan apartment complexes on both sides of the avenue. Larrabee Heights. Fairchild's luxury liner found a curb. Max parked his Ford fifty feet behind and killed the engine.

Mr. Fairchild, a fortyish, skinny man at all angles,

wearing a brown suit plus matching fedora, hopped onto the sidewalk. He drew out the prior slip of paper and held it up to a gunmetal sky, squinting at it against the dull façade of a concrete building. He folded it snugly, then sheathed it back into his suit's inner lining.

Fairchild swung the Chrysler's passenger door wide, tossed the jacket on its seat, and fished out a neatly compressed umbrella. Succeeding the click of the lock, he fleetly ambulated to the distal corner (afar from Max) eyeing the numbers on each dun-colored tenement he passed, clenching the weather shield—a cane serving no purpose.

At the last edifice, Fairchild faltered. Without a rearward glance, he disappeared inside.

Three minutes later, Max made his move. He sauntered to the corner, discovered the entrance unlocked—no fuss, no resistance. He darted freely about the place; Fairchild couldn't identify him any-way. The dank second-floor corridor reeked of foul cabbage dunked in lead paint. The stink assailed his nostrils, reminiscent of being trapped in a low-budget aquarium too long.

In front of apartment 2C, Fairchild's umbrella ineloquently leaned, like a forgotten poem grazing the entryway's molding. Originating beyond the wood: laughter—soft, mingled. A man and a woman, comfortable.

Max unveiled a Kodak Bantam Special from his

inner pocket. He furtively snapped a picture of the umbrella and the door bearing the peeling numbers: 2C. Evidence.

The P.I. rotated toward the stairs. His mind whispered, *Too easy.*

★   ★   ★

Halfway down the dirty white wooden stairs, Max unavoidably came chest to face with a brute built like a steel mill, an irascible-looking type. No hat. A three-day jungle of whiskers crawled across beefy jowls. His pectorals swelled as if pumped full of helium. The stink of R.J. Reynolds Camels and perspiration enveloped his rugged frame.

Max offered an innocuous nod. Devoid of courtesy, the man didn't reciprocate. He stood rooted a few steps below, staring up through hooded eyes, akin to a vicious dog used to seeing smaller creatures flinch. The stairwell tightened, encircling them, hardly a pinch of room to pass. Max slunk by stoically, his shoulder brushing the cracked wall.

The sneaky sleuth was one tread shy of the bottom when he heard the growl "Hey, buddy. What's your business here?"

Mr. Weatherbee hesitated at the landing, gingerly spinning on his heel. "Just visiting my aunt," he lied.

The other snorted.

The instant the investigator hit pavement, the memory of the nosy tenant started fading. He wasn't the reason Max began sniffing around this unfamiliar complex; Max didn't have use for any more reasons.

Returning to the driver's seat of the Ford, Max adjusted the rearview, then lit up a Lucky. The Chrysler he'd spied on sat quietly, all chrome and dirty secrets. He figured all he needed was a pic of Fairchild and the dame together; then case closed.

A problem developed. The ox from the stairwell hadn't vanished. A sliver of him tarried in the doorway, barely half of a torso and a slice of shadowed jaw. Max felt the stare even if he couldn't see the lurking eye. Max wondered why the testy man had to meddle in the matter. He took a drag, sluggish and steady. Patience was part of the gig; now he seemed to be getting watched while getting paid to watch.

Protecting your turf? Max smirked inwardly. *Go home, buddy.*

The other stormed to a rusty Chevy pickup, paused on the side step, and bestowed Max one final glimpse; merely enough to make it memorable.

Then the truck rumbled off.

"Thank goodness," Max muttered to an audience of none, flicking ash out the window, waiting for the rain.

Unbeknownst to Max, the clunker circled around the block, creeping up behind him. The jolt hit harder than anything he'd ever felt playing Dodgems—metal crashing into metal. The Ford bucked forward. Max's kisser slammed against the steering wheel ferociously, stars bursting at the edges of his sockets. The cigarette was milled on impact while his fedora sailed across the coupe, landing upon the passenger-side dash.

The dazed gumshoe barely registered the creak of the curbside door swinging open. A sharp thud bloomed upon his posterior skull—a blackjack. Then Max's world went velvet. The hulk, a dead ringer for a rhino, moved quick for his size, heading back to the corner tenement.

Three minutes later, while Max drooled on the wheel, recounting stars under a charcoal sky, a lady owning a broomstick body scrambled barefoot down one flight of fire escape in a panic.

★   ★   ★

Twilight had taken hold of the city as Max Weatherbee gradually blinked back to life from an involuntary siesta. He didn't know which throbbed worse: the apex or base of his skull. Both were compliments of the brute's twin gifts. Max's brains circled like he'd just been tossed from the tilt-a-whirl at Jolly Charlie's amusement park. He gave the vertigo a measured count to thirty.

The corner activity outside the Ford's window, a few hundred feet away, emerged as smeared, mirroring a Monet impressionist painting in the rain. Through the haze, shapes sharpened into uniforms—bluecoats, clustered and idle, trading cigarette smoke and notes.

In the rearview, the rust-bitten Chevy pickup still clung to his bumper, resembling a junkyard leech.

The private dick rolled up both dress shirt sleeves. The drizzle didn't faze him. If he laid eyes on that slab of muscle again, not even a wall of blue would keep his fists holstered. Cuffed or not, the bully had it coming. Ahead, a knot of about thirty onlookers loomed like condensed olives in a can, only to be callously thrust yonder by authority-draped arms. This was the same tenement Mr. Fairchild had conspicuously slipped into maybe an hour earlier. Max squinted amid the wet and noise. *Does this tie to Fairchild? The animal? Or both?* The question sizzled in his gut, ready to ignite.

Amongst the fracas, behind the rope on the non-civilian section, Max spotted a friend since high school, Officer Freddie Brooks. Brooks, Black and handsome, stood as tall as Max, yet leaner. He carried a dense head of dark hair under his regulation cap, featuring a side fade, no mustache. Similar to Max, he'd also served in the U.S. Army.

The officer halted his colloquy with his portly peer.

"Weatherbee?" a bewildered Brooks greeted, making a don't-come-any-closer motion. "Long time no see."

Seeing his pal mollified Max's anger. He let out a short, relieved breath. "We gotta grab some beers soon, Freddie."

"Sure. What the hell happened to your face, man?"

"Cheap shot."

Officer Brooks peeked cautiously over his muscular shoulder. "Hey, Max," he warned, pointing a long finger, "don't let McGann see you; he's inside."

Max didn't want to see Detective McGann, especially not while displaying a bruised phiz.

"What happened up there, Freddie?"

"A crazy cat came home to find a man in his kitchen where his wife's supposed to be," Brooks divulged, pitching a low tone. "He cut the guy up into pieces using a butcher knife. The gal bolted. Husband's up there now, in restraints. Took five of us to hold him down."

Max slipped furtively into the shadows. Within seconds, he keenly observed the same brute who had attacked him, now cuffed and being led roughly to a squad car. The killer was shoved forward by a hatless man in his late forties, two inches taller than Max, showcasing jagged teeth, a buzz cut, and a wrinkled suit.

The rectangular-faced fellow with flat cheeks was Detective McGann, a man who didn't consider Max's existence on this planet to be of any benefit.

When it seemed reasonable, Max returned to Freddie Brooks.

"Freddie, at least tell me this. What apartment did all the ruckus happen in?"

"2C, Max. 2C."

Max reckoned the police hadn't pegged the Chrysler to Fairchild yet. He inched his Ford off the grizzly's pickup, merely enough for both bumpers to jolt apart creating a metallic snap. He stalled the engine, stepped into the sprinkle, and eyed the dent, wondering if Mrs. Fairchild's expense money might cover the damage. The amusing thought made him chuckle.

A penurious mutt sniffed around Max's pants as he popped the trunk. He gave the poor pooch a swift pet on its head for sympathy. After a quick rummage past the jack and tire iron, the sleuth pulled out a length of wire. A moment later, Reginald Fairchild's Chrysler clicked open, silent and smooth. He'd done this a dozen times, maybe more.

Max fished the deceased man's note from the suit jacket pocket; the one that had meant a whole lot more while its owner was still breathing.

It presented as stark. No signature, no pizazz. Just a bit of scribble, something a finder might toss back on the ground. He read it, then shook his skull, rain tracing along his temple.

Doesn't add up, the private dick mused. *Not yet.*

*   *   *

A day slid by. A newspaper lay unfurled on Max's desk. Under the forever-buzzing fluorescent light, donned in a midnight blue suit, he studied it.

LARRABEE HEIGHTS CARVING
Jealous Husband Nabbed in Love Triangle Slaying
Sonny Torkelson Charged with Murder After Grisly Scene;
Wife Gloria Tied to Suspected Affair
— Mr. Torkelson No Stranger to Neighborhood Violence,
Locals Say —

Meanwhile, in Midtown, a pair of immaculate white wing-tipped shoes guided a white-suited six-foot-four, slender, scar-cheeked hatless man sporting blonde hair parted perfectly down the center into a grimy storefront called Three Kings Pawn.

The owner, a squat, half-bald individual owning eyes akin to pumpkin seeds, locked the door behind the dapper beanpole.

The lanky man spoke first, his drawl purposely sluggish, filled with impertinence. "So, what's the good word, Simon?"

The proprietor responded, sweat pouring down his greasy forehead, "Diamonds, Slick. Diamonds."

★   ★   ★

Back in Old Downtown, Margaret Fairchild showed up late again. Predictable, a clock that ran on lipstick and blitheness. Ursula, the hole-in-the-wall's ancient secretary, ushered her past the threshold in a lackadaisical manner. The widow stood in Max's tidy office, dressed more conservatively this visit, yet the same cloying perfume still clung to the dreary walls.

"My condolences, Mrs. Fairchild," he said, rising to her level, voice monotone, but polite; solicitous. He stood stiffly, hands pressed against the polished desk, his posture rigid as if bracing for a blow to his wallet.

Her mascaraed eyes surrendered to a slow blink. "Mr. Weatherbee, thank you for confirming what I already knew."

Margaret just lost her husband; however, beyond the sheer veil draped over her visage beneath a black mourning hat, she evinced no apparent sorrow. Max didn't contest it.

"Sorry it ended the way it did," he remarked, gesturing to the chair using an open palm. "I'll put together a summary of—"

"Don't bother." Still standing, she coolly glanced toward the seat, then with a small twitch of her head, said "Keep the retainer."

There existed a flicker of impatience beneath her composed exterior, but the words were music to his ears. *A new bumper*, he thought. Maybe even shake hands with a couple of overdue bills. The smile stayed in his pocket.

Upon Mrs. Fairchild's exit, the air in the room had a strange texture—dense, unmoving. A pall of doubt hung alongside her presentation: too poised, too rehearsed, no tears. Max figured he'd peel off twenty smackers from the pot and have his favorite thug shadow the widow, just to see if grief ever made an appearance.

★   ★   ★

Margaret Fairchild moved down the sidewalk like a woman possessing Sunday secrets, buttoned tight in a charcoal gray gabardine number that clung well enough to suggest what it didn't show. The hem flirted with her calves, heels clicking as if they didn't ever walk on dirt. Her bleach blonde hair caught the midday rays, an odd flash of brightness amid the dank crevices of McKinley Avenue. She hauled a compact turquoise valise.

A hundred feet in the distance, keeping lax with pedestrian flow, trailed Max's street hound. He was Giovanni Severoni to his mother; but known to the world as Johnny Knuckles. One coat pocket cradled a set of brass knuckles; the other, a small Kodak Bantam, tucked away with sufficient care to remain unseen.

Johnny Knuckles was a jack-of-all-illegal-trades, making a few bucks running tips, running his mouth, and hustling pool. The private investigator's professional relationship with the scofflaw stretched back to the pre-war days, when Max worked for his uncle Harry Weatherbee's detective agency. The arrangement was simple: Johnny forked over information for a price, and Mr. Weatherbee never shared case details with the ruffian. Today, Johnny planned to be on Mrs. Fairchild's tail, his compensation guaranteed by Max—twenty clams for two days of spying.

Johnny stood just under six feet tall, around thirty, owning a face darker than most fellow Caucasians. His slick ebony hair was combed back, and perched atop it sat a crumpled porkpie hat, worn rearwards; a message to society that he rejected it. A thick gold chain dangled from a solid neck—the kind he couldn't afford to insure—and a weathered black leather jacket rode his shoulders. Beneath, a white tank top hugged a wiry physique, while tan cotton pants draped loose above brown work boots which looked as though they'd stomped more than their share of trouble.

Johnny trailed Margaret Fairchild through Midtown New Paris until she slid into a rundown shop marked *Three Kings Pawn*. The gold paint on the windows was deteriorated and uninviting. From across the street, the hood raised the camera, then snapped a few shots as she stepped inside.

Within the miasmal hock house, Simon—the pint-sized owner—seemed to be expecting her. For privacy, he rotated the lock behind her with a casual twist and quipped, "Nice to see you again, Miss Margaret, seeing I don't know your last name. Understand I had to bring in an associate to raise that kind of dough."

"Better be big bills like I asked. I'm not lugging bags outta here," she snarled dismissively, pointing a polished thumb over a shoulder toward the street.

"Yes, he's aware. But you'll need to leave the ice here. Come back in an hour. He must do a full inspection. You can't see his face; he won't allow it."

"What choice do I have? The cops'll be searching for the goods shortly. However, double-cross me, and you'll meet my dead husband's heater." She nudged the gat's handle out of her purse.

"I'll give you a sizable down payment now. The rest in sixty minutes. No need for threats, ma'am." He leaned over the counter. "Is that revolver for sale by chance?"

The reciprocating glare wasn't pleasant.

Johnny, unable to hear the conversation, crossed traffic and crept to the window's edge. Through the glass, between the interior security bars, he watched Margaret set her valise on the counter, then unfasten it via a thrust. The sleazy man produced a loupe and brought it to one eye, squinting into a tiny lens as he examined the contents. Diamonds, obvious to peeping Johnny. The merchant took his time, nodding periodically, languid and deliberate.

Five minutes later, Margaret briskly flipped through a stack of greenbacks, leaving the unwanted case and gems abandoned. She exited with her chin high and mighty; her pocketbook a little fatter, the mystery a little deeper.

Simultaneously Johnny, now a city block away, snapped another image.

Mrs. Fairchild's next stop was a joint called O'Rourke's, a narrow saloon housing filthy mirrors, bad lighting, and a floor that hadn't seen a mop since

Prohibition. The air hung thick, radiating stale beer and peanuts.

At the far end of the bar sat a plain woman, unfamiliar to Johnny but about the same age as Margaret Fairchild, all frail frame and sharp edges. Johnny didn't know her name; didn't need to know it was Gloria Torkelson. Didn't need to know her husband, Sonny, was facing a murder rap. But it would've helped to know she was the ghost Max missed two nights ago, slipping down a fire escape while he was knocked out cold like a Joe Louis opponent.

What mattered was Johnny heard her scold the other woman, "Whatta you mean, you left 'em there?" Whispering followed, tense and urgent.

Johnny muttered a few grumbles to a buzzard-faced bartender, then slid him a fin—the kind he reckoned Max would square later.

Behind the bar, Johnny ditched his biker jacket. He then posted near the sink, playing the part of a chump working under the table, suds up to his elbows, close enough to catch the ladies' chatter.

When they clocked him, he tossed a lazy grin. "*Hola.*"

Mrs. Fairchild flashed him the once-over, nose wrinkling. "We don't require anything right now."

Johnny wasn't Mexican, but he could sell the part for a matinee and a dime. "*No hablo inglés,*" he blurted, then slouched back to his pointless duties.

The ruse worked. The ladies relaxed, megrims vanished, voices lowering.

"You sold that stuff for forty percent of what it's worth," Gloria Torkelson spat, her inflection bitter. "And we don't even have all the cash yet."

Mrs. Fairchild gazed anew at Johnny, who was scrubbing the faucet as if it were an Old English sheepdog.

"We will in an hour," she snipped at Gloria. "It's plenty to live on for five years."

"Agreed."

"We killed," Margaret Fairchild intoned, gripping her wine goblet, "two birds with one stone."

"No more being told what to do," Torkelson added, lifting hers.

"One bird's dead, the other's in a prison coop," murmured the black widow. "Let's drink to us."

Glasses clinked—a crisp, brittle sound.

Johnny's scouring, homemade-tattooed arms told him the sink was clean. He'd procured sufficient grist to earn the assured twenty dollars. Time to phone Max.

*   *   *

At Max's office, the overhead light buzzed irritably, echoing an electric razor caught in stubble. His size twelve dress shoes rested on the expansive desk, ankles crossed, while the city breathed hard through the lone open window.

Ursula's voice crackled hoarsely via the intercom. "Freddie Brooks is calling, Max."

The sleeves of the sleuth's white shirt were rolled up to his elbows. His suit jacket and fedora hung like ghosts on the coat-tree in the corner.

He picked up the receiver, voice clipped. "Max Weatherbee."

Brooks came in coolly over the wire. "Max, it's Freddie. Story's about to break. Figured you'd wanna piece. I saw you pokin' around Larrabee Heights. I know you're straight."

"I appreciate that, Freddie."

The patrolman didn't dally. "The butchered banker, Reginald Fairchild, was in cahoots with a crooked locksmith by the name of Dennehy. Dennehy is currently singing at the precinct as we speak."

The excitement in Max's nerves had him deftly spark up a Lucky Strike as he listened.

"Fairchild frequently let Dennehy into the safe deposit vault," Freddie went on. "Signed him in as if he was a legit box holder. Found what renters were stashing diamonds and other gems. Between Fairchild's bank key and Dennehy's skills, they were looting the joint clean."

Max exhaled smoke languidly. "It's starting to come together. Let me guess: Sonny Torkelson, the one sitting in a frigid cell, never even met Fairchild before the macabre moment."

"McGann's trying to sort that out. Max, if you

possess something you gotta bring it to him. It's the right thing."

"I will," Max said, the words drifting in the haze.

Freddie lowered his voice gravely. "Thing is, what was Fairchild doin' alone in Torkelson's apartment? It's the part that doesn't track."

"Alone?"

"Torkelson swears his wife wasn't home when he found the banker there."

The PI narrowed his eyes toward the glum wall, at a picture of his high school football team. "Freddie, I heard two voices," he imparted flatly, "behind the door of unit 2C. And one of 'em sure as hell wasn't a man."

* * *

While the dames were chiming glasses in celebration, a pair of bone-white wingtips ominously glided across the cracked tile of Three Kings Pawn. Slick, the tall drink of menace in a chalk suit, was making his second visit.

The place reeked of mothballs and yesterday's chicken soup, which some say is one and the same as armpit odor. Shelves buckled under the weight of junk no one had wanted in a decade: rusty relics, outdated banjo clocks, and a saxophone, green with neglect.

Simon, the runty proprietor, looked similar to one of Snow White's lesser-known goons, standing beside the spiffy man. As usual, when it was crunch time for real business, Simon scurried, locked the establishment's main door, then dimmed the lights.

He shuffled to the counter. "Slick, this is the last of the diamonds," he muttered, his voice pitched low, obedient.

Slick reached out one gangly arm, fingers resembling pincers, and gave the dealer's thinning scalp a nonchalant rub. "Time for a rug, don'tcha think, Simon?"

Simon chuckled; not because it was funny, but because it was smart. "Slick, I handed her all the cash you fronted me. She's coming back soon for the rest."

It served as a sarcastic plaudit. "You did well, Simon." The scar that split Slick's cheek tugged tight during each utterance, his tone dead as a tombstone.

Simon eased Margaret Fairchild's valise onto a glass display case, popped it open, and started sifting through the stones, creating a neat, separate pile.

"I'm makin' a stack," the merchant murmured, "for my effort, as we agreed."

Slick peered low at the mound, offered a malevolent grin, and remarked sardonically, "Your heap's girth is gettin' a tad unreasonable, don'tcha think?"

"You promised to be fair, Slick," the shrimp pleaded.

The shadows precisely hit Slick's sinister mug, a prelude for his next course of action. He turned to glance out the front window—no movement, no

witnesses—then spun back around. The Luger slid
into his hand, smooth as jazz.

"Promises," the racketeer drawled, his voice deadpan, "are like donkey shit, Simon. Dirty when you
step in 'em."

⋆   ⋆   ⋆

Johnny and his black leather jacket skulked away
from O'Rourke's, leaving behind the two loose-lipped
ladies, alongside their mountain of cigarette butts.
The jukebox crooned something slow as he stepped
purposefully into the sunlight, palms jammed deep in
his pockets. Next stop: a public library. He needed to
make good on a favor Max had requested.

Inside the gold-domed structure, polished floors
squeaked beneath his boots as if they were tattling.
Every Bookmark Benny and Card Catalog Clara
swiveled to gawk; some with squints, others with
suspicion. Leather wasn't standard issue among the
cardigan crowd. He didn't belong and attempted no
effort to pretend to the contrary.

The reference area lay as quiet as a funeral home
during a blizzard. The hood efficiently dug up the
1935 high school yearbook he'd been searching for.

A small sign hung sternly on the wall resembling
a courtroom verdict: "NO PRINTED MATERIAL
MAY BE REMOVED FROM THIS SECTION."

Knuckles smirked. He was able to read—though
not write—and rule-breaking seemed imbued in his

livelihood. Exhibiting insouciance, mimicking an unscrupulous street magician, he nimbly stuffed the library's property between his ribs and his white T-shirt. Soon, he was gone like Babe Ruth's booze cruises.

Elsewhere, wine-buzzed Margaret Fairchild and Gloria Torkelson made their way down the block. Gloria, decked in a sales rack special from Woolworth's—rayon and a little desperation—trailed just behind Margaret, who dressed akin to a B movie queen, catching the ogling peepers of a few married men.

Inside the musty pawn shop, seeing no one tending to the counter, Margaret called out, smug and sharp, "Simon, I'm back!"

What answered wasn't a voice, but a stillness too heavy for the hour. One step farther and they spotted him: Simon, crumpled beyond the display case, a discarded marionette, glassy eyes open, gape in the forehead. Blood spatter clung to the walls, congruent to those fuzzy things nobody ever remembered the name of under a microscope in tenth-grade science class.

Platinum-tressed Margaret shrieked first—thunderstruck. Gloria followed suit, and in the subsequent beat, the women frantically tore out of the joint in opposite directions.

★   ★   ★

Twilight set in over the city like a gradual leak. Max stalled his Ford coupe against the curb; same spot where the brute had ambushed him a few days ago. No blindside tonight. The jealous spouse was behind bars, donned in state-issued threads.

The masculine PI lit up a Lucky, ambled to the corner, and climbed splintered stairs. Apartment 2C. He knocked three times, sharp.

"Who's there?" came a woman's voice from beyond the pine, taut in a lattice of nerves.

"The super sent me," Max lied.

The door swung open with fury. Waifish Gloria Torkelson stood attentively. Simple dress, flat shoes, brown hair twisted into curlers beneath a kerchief. Homestyle glamour, the kind which could ward off male spirits.

"The rent's paid," she stated coolly.

"Name's Max Weatherbee. Private dick. I've got questions."

"Stop right there. You cross that threshold, I scream."

"I'll stay planted."

"I told the fuzz," she spat, swinging her arms, "all I knew, which was nothing, besides that I'd been having an affair with Reginald Fairchild and my nutso husband found out. Please leave."

To Max, it dripped out too smooth, echoing a routine she'd practiced in the mirror. He didn't budge.

"Answer me this," the operative pressed. "How long was the tryst going on for?"

"Same line I told the cops: six months."

"Six months, huh? Knowing your better half's explosive fuse, wouldn't this place be risky for a rendezvous of infidelity?"

"Reggie," she growled, topaz eyes glowering, "frequently stopped by when Sonny was working. That day, the lug got off early, unexpectedly."

"Yeah, I met Sonny right before he carved Fairchild up like Thanksgiving turkey," Max disclosed, tipping his fedora back to show a violet contusion blooming at his hairline. "See?"

Gloria winced. "What'd you do to make him irate?"

"Shadowing Fairchild, ma'am. I'm guessing your hubby figured I was paying you a love visit and decided to send a vengeful message."

"I don't have much else to say," she snapped, inching toward the door.

He smiled mirthlessly. "Three things don't sit right, Mrs. Torkelson. First: oddly, you actually answered my inquiries as if you were expecting me. Second: the salvage yard says your husband frequently clocks out prior to his quitting hour. And third—"

Her hand gripped the knob, cutting him off. "Get the hell outta here!" she yelled.

Unwavering, he planted his size twelve Roblee against the wood, preventing her from slamming it.

He resumed, "Third: an item which will soon be in the clutches of a city detective named McGann."

He pulled out the note he'd confiscated from Reginald Fairchild's suit jacket and held it high in the air between two thick fingers.

"Ma'am, your address is written on it. Mr. Fairchild was studying it outside. He'd never been here before the afternoon he got snuffed."

The color drained out of Gloria's countenance like someone'd stuck a Hoover vacuum cleaner hose to it.

Max verbalized no more and egressed the low-rent dwelling. Gloria Torkelson stifled a gasp, then hurled a suitcase onto the bed, snatched the receiver from its cradle, and dialed quick.

Three seconds passed. To the mouthpiece she said, "We've been made."

*   *   *

Night had taken over the sky. Max loosened his tie and strode into the eleven-story Kaiser Building—concrete bones, soot-streaked windows. A skyscraper in 1907, but by '47, merely another outdated monolith housing more ghosts than tenants.

In the lobby's desolate coffee shop, he dropped a nickel, and left with a *New Paris Times* evening bulletin tucked firmly under one arm.

The elevator was manned by a postadolescent in a red cap three sizes too big. Max rode up to the ninth floor, killing a minute idly gawking at the headline.

Murdered Banker Tied to Jewel Theft Ring
Safe Deposit Boxes Compromised—Locksmith Accomplice
Held, Seeking Legal Counsel
Police: Fairchild Homicide Likely Unrelated
Detectives Now on Scene in Killing of Three Kings Pawn
Owner Simon Katz

Max blinked once, deliberately, then muttered, "That's a mouthful."

The kid operating the ascending box responded, "Huh?"

When the metal slid open, the sleuth stepped out, pivoted right, and reached for his key. However, someone happened to be blocking the entrance.

Pitching a serious tone, Max said, "Johnny. I was wondering how you made out."

Johnny, garbed in his favorite getup, leaned against the door like it was giving him a heinie massage. "Tried callin' yuh. Gots film an', uh, yearbook. Nineteen thirty-five, Central High. I want my twenty."

Inside his office, Max flipped on the lights, hung up his suit jacket, and casually sparked up a cigarette.

Both men sat. Johnny gave a rundown of what he'd seen on the street and overheard at O'Rourke's. One Andrew Jackson changed hands in exchange for Max's camera and the library property.

The PI grinned dryly. "Johnny, it was supposed to be two days of tailing Mrs. Fairchild."

The hood smirked. "You gots more than twenty worth there, Mr. Bee."

To Max, the mug's loyalty was always infallible. "You're too good to me, Johnny. Stick around five minutes, will you?"

Max leafed through the yearbook, licking his thumb as he slowly turned each page, his eyes scanning faces as if he were lining up suspects. In the graduating seniors section, he folded one page and paused at another.

"Okay, Johnny. They're a little younger here, but are these the two women you saw today? One is now a blonde, though."

Knuckles keenly examined the photos Max pointed at. "Yep. One of 'em looks duh same—duh skinny one."

"Thanks, Johnny."

"Whatcha," the ruffian asked, pointing a greasy finger, "gonna do wit' dat yearbook, Mr. Bee? It's mine—I stole it."

Max raised a brow. "It's going back to the reference desk, Johnny. And if I trusted you a little more, you'd be the one doing the returning."

They both laughed. Johnny slipped out. Max took the film into the darkroom.

*   *   *

The next morning, the sleuth was gingerly taking a batch of photos from the darkroom. Suddenly, droopy-eyed police detective Dan McGann showed up, and the office felt a lot smaller when he did. The visit came at Max's request; one that wouldn't put any money in his pocket. Ursula, as silent as a shadow in a forgotten alley, let him in.

McGann, a broad-shouldered man owning a boxy frame, boasted a good fifteen years on Max. He stood tall enough that you could picture him throwing fast-balls in a minor league uniform years ago. His close-cropped gray hair bristled defiantly above a crooked sneer, and the suit clinging to him looked like it hadn't left his body in forty-eight hours.

"I'm a busy person, Weatherbee. If I'm here, it's outta respect for your Uncle Harry; best damn investigator the department had when I was green," McGann growled, raising a chunky finger. "Taught me more than I wanted to know. Don't think for a second I'm nursing a soft spot for private dicks."

"Uncle Harry eventually became one," Max responded wryly, aware it wouldn't score him points.

"Yeah, after he hung up the badge. Whatcha got, Weatherbee? We're holding two dames at the station based on your phone call last night. This better be good, or I'll pull your license faster than Oliver Hardy can inhale a one-gallon bowl of Manhattan chowder."

Max bit his lip. The two hatless men in dark suits sat across from one another.

"Had to wait for the photos to dry so bear with me, Dan," Max urged, dropping several images on the desk. Shots of Margaret slipping in and out of Three Kings Pawn. A couple of pics of her jawing alongside Simon Katz came out grainy—the ones Johnny'd snapped through the window. McGann picked them up, squinting.

"I'm listening," the police detective muttered superciliously.

The P.I. orated, "Here's how it goes. Margaret Fairchild and Gloria Torkelson: old high school pals. They lost touch. One had money—college, married a banker, the smooth road. The latter bounced from job to job, wound up wed to a scrapyard foreman. Life dealt 'em different hands, but somewhere along the line, they reconnected. And decided to trade favors. Kill each other's problems. Namely, their husbands."

McGann grunted. Max went on.

"Margaret fancied hers six feet deep. He was stealing jewels. You know this; lifting them straight from safe deposit boxes with the assistance of a locksmith gone sour."

"Yup. The crooked keyman's in custody," McGann remarked, his voice hoarse.

Max resumed the dirt. "The loot is worth a fortune. Margaret knew where her spouse stashed his cut and figured once it was hers, she'd be sittin' pretty. Easy street, all laid out. See, by way of poking around, I learned Reginald lived as a degenerate gambler and Margaret figured that grab would be as good as gone."

McGann's bloodshot eyes widened. "Okay, which

explains why a banker would choose to take such a risk."

Max further encapsulated the wicked scheme. "Now flip the coin: Gloria's husband, Sonny, is a beast. Kept her under his thumb, made her existence hell. So, the two lassies cooked up a caper. Margaret told her hubby Reginald that Gloria was circlin' the drain, suicidal. Said even though he didn't know her, he oughta check in on her. He took the bait, went over there following work."

McGann placed a massive elbow on the desk and cupped his square chin with big fingers, taking it all in.

Max further elaborated, "I was tailing him. Margaret Fairchild slipped me a retainer, swearing he'd been stepping out on her. Claimed she wanted proof of his cheating. Funny thing is, after the gig, she let me keep the whole retainer. No questions, no weeping. Ain't nobody that generous, not in this town. Obviously, her plan was for me to serve as a witness to his supposed cheating, figuring that would be the end of it."

McGann huffed. "Go on, Weatherbee."

"Anyway, Sonny Torkelson, the possessive type, came home in a blind rage, just as the ladies anticipated, and butchered poor ol' Reginald Fairchild. Gloria was in their apartment entertaining the banker, but Sonny, once they hauled him in, claimed she wasn't. Not sure why. Maybe the maniac is simply protecting her."

"Sounds right," agreed the lawman.

"With both hubbies out of the picture, the dames began hocking the gems. Everything was going smooth until the pawn shop proprietor turned up dead. They also didn't plan on the bank discovering the heist so quickly and linking it to Mr. Fairchild, a model employee. Also, I don't think the frails got all the money they were supposed to, because my associate listened in on their conversation at O'Rourke's. They must've been stiffed."

"Thanks to your concerned citizen intel, we found a decent stash on Mrs. Fairchild," McGann divulged. "Yet nowhere near the full value. Just enough to give us probable cause to detain her. We caught her on a promenade, pulling luggage, trying to hail a hack. The diamonds are missing, and we've got an open homicide: Simon Katz, owner of Three Kings Pawn."

"Yeah, I don't think they killed him," Max theorized. "If they had, they'd be sittin' on a grander haul. More cash, more stones."

"Could be," McGann nodded grudgingly. "Either way, your snapshots are gonna help us nail 'em on something. Seeing as Katz won't be testifying anytime soon."

Max lit up a Lucky. Using his fingers, he offered one to his austere visitor, who shook his head. The PI's smoke swirled between them.

McGann rasped, "Neither one is leaving the damn precinct. After your late-night tip, we also picked up the lovely Gloria at the train station on the grounds she was warned not to leave town. Won't be long now. They'll start squawking on each other, and that squawking will seal both their coffins."

"You do have a knack for that, don't you, McGann?"

"Sure do. And don't you ever wind up on the wrong side of the tracks."

Max blew smoke. "Why don't you like me, Dan?"

"Because I don't like people. Any people."

Max let out a dry chuckle. "What's happening to Sonny Torkelson?"

"Might get the chair for murder."

"The world's safer without him."

"You know him?"

Max pointed upward at the bruise.

"Don't you think it's time to find another line of work, Weatherbee?"

*   *   *

In a plush apartment thirty miles north of New Paris, in a city called Adamsville, Slick Peterson—six-foot-four and built for speed—dropped a folded newspaper on the kitchen table. The scar running down his cheek twitched as his eyes settled on the front-page headline:

Devious Female Duo Margaret Fairchild and Gloria Torkelson Charged with Conspiracy in the Homicide of Reginald Fairchild
Sonny Torkelson Pleads Guilty to Murder, Punches Guards in the Meantime—Chair Probable
Slain Pawn Shop Owner Simon Katz; Police Say Case Unrelated, No Suspects

Beside the paper sat Margaret's valise, bulging with precious stones. Slick leaned rearward, a slanted grin crawling across his face, the kind of grin a man would exhibit when he'd gotten away with both the murder and the ice.

The End.

Look for the return of Max Weatherbee, Detective McGann, Freddie Brooks, Johnny Knuckles, and the sinister Slick in Allan Kevorkian's full-length novel *No Escape from Death*. Available now.

6

THEY WON'T HURT YOU

It was a humid September 1947 afternoon in Lafayette, Louisiana. The kind of day when your undergarments serve as a sponge, soaking up the body's salty sweat. The kind of day when a Coca-Cola sign swaying atop a diner called Bernie's Cajun certainly would've tickled one's fancy.

A timeworn '35 Chevrolet—the type with the thin grille—rumbled on the outskirts of town in an area where oak and cypress trees seemed plentiful. Their branches stretched forth, warning of dark secrets they couldn't verbalize.

Seeing the Coke advertisement, the three Crane sisters, approaching middle age and traveling together, cut their jalopy's engine and languidly drifted into the joint. Bernie's door was propped open, welcoming neighborhood flies or anyone else searching for a bite to eat. Inside, one ceiling fan creaked ominously, swirling echoes of greasy, overcooked meals and half-finished conversations. Seven lost souls were dotted about; including, at the counter's far end, a burly man displaying a sheriff's badge, sitting heavy, looking like he owned the room.

The three dark brown-haired siblings reached the counter, their block heels echoing loudly along the way. They sat in sequence, left to right, in order of age.

Eleanor, on the left, was a slender woman with a short bob hairstyle featuring soft waves, slightly tousled and parted to the left. Her cheeks stuck out, resembling two pears rotated sideways with their points nearly touching at the nose's bridge. She carried green eyes, keen as the wind, unveiling dreams of distant horizons.

In the middle idly lingered Grace Crane, sporting a petite pillbox hat that made the girth of her pudgy head appear even bigger. Her vast, ocean-blue eyes were wondrous.

Ann Crane sat on the right. She had a flat face and hair pompadoured up top, with bushy sides below.

The trio wore simple house dresses of the type you'd find in a low-end department store.

To the server, Ann, the gregarious sibling, animatedly remarked, sticking up a petite nose, "It's hotter in here than outside."

The thick-waisted waitress, wearing a yellow apron, took an unscheduled rendezvous from fanning her perspiring face. Her honey-brown hair was neatly tucked into a bun. "Yep, sugar. What else is on yer mind?"

"Three Cokes." Ann's voice was always squeaky.

"And?"

"Any recommendations," Ann asked, "for pie?"

"Pecan." A husky rasp coated her southern drawl, drowning out the overhead fan. "Obviously, y'all ain't native tuh these parts."

"Well, no ma'am...we owned ourselves a farm up in Spencer, Indiana. Now we're traveling with my big sister Eleanor. She's got a knack for penning ghost stories." Ann's innocent tone carried the verve of someone who had yet to endure hardship. The talker continued, "I'm her stenographer, and Grace here is the secretary. She keeps our wheels greased."

"Name's Flo. I reckon I never heard of yuh," the waitress grumbled, her umber eyes giving Eleanor Crane an incredulous, unwanted inspection.

"Well," Eleanor disclosed, politely staring, "it's because my tales haven't really gone national yet."

"I see," Flo muttered, as if she cared, noticing the air of coyness in the ghost writer.

Ann Crane hogged the floor again. "We came down here seeking to rent an old mansion for a year, preferably one that's rumored to be inhabited by spirits. A haven where Eleanor can write stories."

The waitress, expelling a laugh like a broken jukebox, pointed a broad finger toward an elongated, dirty commercial window. "Yuh can start righ' there yonder by th' lake."

Flo's version of the English language took the sisters a few seconds to process, but her words piqued curiosity. The three Cranes spun around on their red stools. The stools screeched when they did. Across the street, they observed a turret, its conical roof popping its head above tall trees in a mysterious prelude. The rest of the Victorian home was hidden from view. The trio spun back in unison, as if all of their movements were in sync.

"I could plant my garden," Grace suggested, speaking for the first time.

Without seeing it, Eleanor sketched the rest of the dwelling in her mind. "Do you know the owner's name?" she inquired to Flo.

"Mr. Landry—well, really Mrs. Landry, and that's a whole 'nother tale." Then Flo furtively whispered, "Place is haunted."

"Why are you whispering?" questioned Ann, puzzled.

"Cuz Sheriff Dugas yonder don't buhlieve in no ghosts."

The three gals gawked at the lawman. Chomping on a thick cigar, he reciprocated a glance over a newspaper, which was lying atop a dirty plate. He presented as a portly, double-chinned man, balancing a broad-brimmed hat. The armpits of his tan uniform appeared dampened. His eyes soon grew uninterested.

To the middle sister, Grace, Flo dryly quipped, "Yuh ain't much of a talker, hon." She pushed a plate of pie in front of her customer. "Yuh buhlieve in ghosts?"

"Nope."

The women hurried up and ate.

On the way out, Bernie's seven patrons heard Ann, the youngest and most loquacious of the departing sisters, say, "This might be perfect!"

The sheriff's meaty lips formed a sly smirk before he gauchely burped up a quart of gastric acid.

To the out-of-towners' hindside, Flo's phiz cast a cynical look.

★   ★   ★

The next day, at the foot of a graveled driveway, a battered "For Rent" sign leaned, like it had given up hope long ago, its letters barely legible from the road. At the end of the driveway, past towering cypress trees, stood a neglected, faded gray dwelling, having lost its majesty since the reign of Queen Victoria. Its bay window jutted out, as if it were pushing intruders away.

A veranda wrapped around the house, its surrounding balustrade peeling, mimicking an undesirable sunburn. A polygonal window in the home's center gave the impression of an ominous, unblinking, peeping eye. The structure bore three floors. The first two were stacked identically on its outside, while the asymmetrical third whispered trouble.

Mrs. Landry, a striking, fortyish lady possessing rakish charm, leisurely sauntered hither and thither, traversing the gravel. She paused, glancing toward the lake, either to admire it or pretend to, for the potential tenants browsing the interior structure.

Her blonde locks featured victory rolls, half up, half down. She was donned in a snug-fitting salmon pink peplum dress that hugged her curves, paired with black pumps that clicked at every step. A gaudy, chandelier-beaded necklace rested upon Landry's neckline. She wore plenty of rouge over an already attractive face.

Inside the bay window's spacious alcove, Eleanor's mind spoke in a smoky, wistful tone. *I've just got to do my writing here...I can feel their presence.*

The other two gals darted erratically from room to room, each in her own way exuding jittery urgency, prowling about the place like a cat exploring an alien land.

The furniture was all draped in sheets, forming what it always does—a bunch of ghostly silhouettes, especially the armchairs. When the self-guided tour began to lose its appeal, the three siblings came outside via a pair of archaic, matching double doors.

"How'd you fancy it?" asked Mrs. Landry curiously, halting her beholding of the lake. The Crane sisters noticed the unfamiliar woman lacked a Southern accent.

Resembling a football huddle in a pickup game, the three travelers circled around the landlady.

"It includes all this nice furniture?" Ann asked excitedly, as if she were a kid receiving an extra allowance.

"Yes, the previous tenant left it behind."

"That'll, save us a lot of money," said Eleanor curtly. "So, no need to negotiate on the price."

Mrs. Landry's nod indicated she appreciated what she heard.

"Why didn't you come inside with us?" Ann queried, rocking her torso, unable to stand still.

"I sort of let the property sell itself," the diva imparted, forcing a painted smile. "I'm not a pushy type."

"We'll take it," announced the author.

"Not so fast," countered Mrs. Landry, jutting a claret nail at Eleanor, understanding she had control. "I require the payment in cash, a minimum of one year."

Eleanor's eyes secretly admired the debonair woman's aesthetic quality, plus confidence. She found it both attractive and unfamiliar, introspectively wondering why.

"Can't do month to month?" bartered Grace, the less talkative sister.

Eleanor inconspicuously poked a bony elbow

into Grace's beefy lower ribs, then divulged to Mrs. Landry, "I have the money in my suitcase."

"There's no refunds," Landry intoned portentously.

The sisters nodded, knowing the weight of the decision would settle on Eleanor's shoulders. Then they heard the crunch of gravel.

Walking up the path from the lake's dock was a skinny man, owning dark hair that cascaded down, partially covering generously lobed ears. The stranger's Adam's apple protruded like the real fruit. His gaunt, bristly mug squinted against the bright Louisiana sun.

A weathered straw hat crowned the poor fellow's head, casting a shadow over bloodshot eyes, while a toothpick lazily poked out of a corner of a twisted mouth. His patchwork flannel shirt, sun-bleached and well-worn, hung loosely beneath a khaki-colored fishing vest, its large pockets bulging with trinkets of the trade. A pair of loose beige trousers were supported by suspenders, the cuffs rolled up merely enough to reveal scuffed brown boots.

The three siblings rubbed shoulders, their movements stiff with unease at the stranger's slow, creeping encroachment.

"Oh, by the way," disclosed Mrs. Landry smugly, "this is Felix; he fixes things." She offered a mirthless smile. "He's at your service."

"Hul...lo." His Louisianan drawl aired creepier than his treacherous appearance.

Eleanor peered into Felix's dark eyes; they were vacant, missing an "Out to Lunch" sign.

Thirty minutes later, sitting erect on a round padded stool at Bernie's Cajun, Mrs. Landry picked through her black clutch bag.

"One coffee, Flo," she said.

"I only see that grin," Flo replied knowingly, serving a mug of hot coffee, "when yuh rent the place."

"Yes, to the three ugly ducklings," cackled Mrs. Landry.

Flo herself guffawed obnoxiously enough to be the loudest thing in the room. "I saw 'em. Sent 'em y'all's way."

To the right of the establishment's lengthy counter, Sheriff Dugas looked on, showcasing inquisitiveness. His belly bloated with ample cooking grease to resemble a piñata before the first kid strikes it.

Prior to exiting, Mrs. Landry dropped a five-dollar bill atop the counter. It wasn't a tip.

*   *   *

Steering using pristine white gloves, Mrs. Landry guided her zipping yellow Lincoln Zephyr coupe to its second stop halfway to downtown: a shabby fisherman's dive on the Vermilion River lacking an advertising sign that Lafayette locals called the Foxhole.

Several shanties in the periphery exhibited paint wear. The outside air carried a tart, earthen scent, rich with a muddled odor of damp soil. Inside, the joint reeked of fish. The dump's denizens were immune to it, but the eloquent Mrs. Landry, high heels clacking, started pinching her nose. The few male regulars sinking in sorrow didn't seem too excited about her entrance; they knew her destination.

At the bar, a head familiar to her slumped onto an outstretched arm—a poor man's substitute for a feather pillow. The drunkard appeared four days unshaven, a moderate-sized individual carrying thin, straggly blonde hair that barely covered a bald cranium, mirroring a radio's circuit board.

She flicked his ear, employing a gloved index finger.

Mrs. Landry's pathetic, florid-faced husband temporarily winced and sat up straight on the barstool, but then his body started teetering—a dead ringer for a carnival shooting gallery target. She cast him the apathetic gawk a callous woman gave a houseplant she'd forgotten to water for weeks.

Before fishing in her handbag, she adjusted the silk gloves on slender fingers, her jagged nails protruding like tiny daggers in the dull light.

"Here's a few bucks," she hissed impassively, tossing three crumpled George Washington portraits onto the bar as if they were worth less than the ink that printed them.

"Heard...from a fly on the wall...some folk...been lookin' at the estate." Mr. Landry's slurred words sounded like his tongue was glued to his hard palate. "Why only...three bucks?"

"Because you can't be trusted with money," she chided, disdaining his supplication, flicking his ear once more. "Go ahead, make yourself even drunker. If not for me, you'd be livin' in a Hooverville. Make sure you sleep on the couch when you get home. You stink."

Mr. Landry unsteadily raised a half-full whisky glass. "To Herbert Hoover," he inanely slurred.

"Whatever." Mrs. Landry cared to hear no more and departed as briskly as she came in.

One sleek Lincoln purred its way into inner-city Lafayette. After parking, Mrs. Landry ostentatiously strolled through the heart of the city, dropping cash akin to leaves falling to the earth on a New Hampshire autumn day. A man noticed—a corpulent one, spying with sharp eyes, lurking in a big Ford sedan. Prominent writing on its doors read *Sheriff's Department, Lafayette Parish.*

*   *   *

Back inside the home on the lake, the three Crane sisters went about removing the sheets covering the furniture and taking pictures, wielding a black Kodak camera.

"Why would someone abandon all these nice fixtures?" Ann murmured, her voice dripping in naïveté.

"That's something we're going to deduce," replied Eleanor, speaking like a sleuth.

Grace and Ann stood rooted in place, mimicking statues in a gallery of apprehension.

Hours later, an indigo sky surrendered to the encroaching darkness. Eleanor was settled, scribbling musings for her next novel. Meanwhile, Ann peeked out a rear window and became frightened. A moving light hovered over the lake, drifting closer to shore with each passing second. Her pulse quickened.

As the light grew nearer, Ann's fear faintly untangled itself. She perceived a small rowboat; a lantern hung from its bow. By way of its glow, she recognized the motorless skiff's operator as the eerie stranger she'd crossed paths with earlier today, a fellow simply introduced as Felix.

Five minutes dragged by like a slow-burning cigarette, then came the knock—heavy as a judge's gavel, each rap landing three seconds apart, echoing with clockwork precision. The siblings exchanged wary glances. Next, all their eyes peeked out the curtainless bay window and saw the obscure figure.

"It's Felix," Ann made known in an attempt to assuage the others.

Grace clutched Eleanor's arm unconsciously, before Eleanor flicked the exterior light on, and together the sisters answered the door.

Felix loitered, offering a baleful expression on his

already tortured countenance. He gravely apprised the trio, "Leeeeave...now, while...yuh still can."

★   ★   ★

In the afternoon rays, the three Cranes stepped out of a Rexall pharmacy, a bell above the glass door jangling loudly as it swung shut behind them. Grace clutched a crisp paper envelope, her chubby fingers rhythmically tapping it against her palm.

In sync, the trio strolled toward a wrought iron bench nestled among some greenery.

To Grace, Ann asked impatiently, "Let's see 'em."

Grace opened the envelope. A dozen images—snapshots of the house, its stately exterior and shadowed interior rooms—made their rounds silently. The gals viewed them, displaying keen interest initially, but their enthusiasm soon waned, the novelty wearing thin.

Ann, the one possessing the uncontainable energy, took hold of the stack while the others enjoyed soda pops until their straws both produced a *sluuuurp*. She reexamined them, putting two photos on top, then raised a brow inquisitively.

"Hey!" Ann exclaimed. "See this?" Her tone aired on the side of fright. She passed a photo to each sister.

"What's the matter?" inquired Eleanor.

"These two pics," Ann imparted, pointing, "are of rooms that contain mirrors."

"A few of the rooms have mirrors," remarked Eleanor, shrugging her delicate shoulders.

"Yes, but closely inspect these two."

"Oh my!" cried Grace, astonished, her round facial features siphoned of color.

Eleanor eagerly snatched them, then examined both side by side.

In each black-and-white picture, a distorted figure could be seen reflected in a mirror, dressed in 1800s attire. One was a man, the other a woman, their upper bodies the only visible part of the reflection. Their mouths were agape, frozen in an eerie, wordless scream.

I knew spirits existed there, mused Eleanor internally, fascinated with the discovery.

★   ★   ★

At a desolate Bernie's Cajun, Flo leaned against the counter, filing her nails with all the urgency of drying paint. Sheriff Dugas was absent from his usual spot, but across the counter, opposite Flo the waitress, sat the sphinxlike, pulchritudinous face of Mrs. Landry.

The flamboyant feline smoked a cigarette, neatly fitted inside a black Bakelite holder. Her carmine-painted lips stained its mouthpiece. She sported a sweetheart neckline on her floral-print, knee-length dress.

The diner stirred to life; three pairs of clunky

shoes shuffled in. Perched similar to crows on a wire, the Crane trio loomed over Mrs. Landry's stool. She gave a petulant frown, not appreciating such an intrusion.

Ann spoke first, practically bouncing on her toes. "Mrs. Landry, Mrs. Landry, you must see these pictures." She then plopped the ghostly snapshots in front of the seated woman.

Landry's voice indignantly thundered, "What?"

"Look," instructed Ann, tapping an index finger on one photo, "at the mirrors in the images."

"Oh, that. They won't hurt you. Seen it before."

Grace spoke, her tone flat like a busted tire. "Are they ghosts?"

"Who knows?" quipped the landlord blithely. "Who cares?"

The only additional patron in the establishment was an older man, owning a mop of unkempt hair, the kind which screamed scientist or madman—sometimes both.

"Lemme see 'em," he muttered.

Mrs. Landry slid them down the worn Formica counter.

The man studied them, squinting through smudged lenses, and theorized, "Yup, them are ghosts all right. Mirrors ain't just for checking your lipstick, ladies; they're portals to their world. It's where our dimensions cross paths."

"This is fascinating," said Ann.

Flo and Mrs. Landry stared at each other, both knowingly trying to contain their laughter.

That night, Grace prepared a suds bath in the claw-foot porcelain tub on the second floor. Prior to easing in, she turned on a tabletop radio resting on a shelf above. Listening to jazz music, a relaxed Grace, in a rare escape from her persistent anxiety, sighed as she descended deeper amidst the warmth. Her fingers floated like a message in a bottle. She closed both eyes, but something made her open them.

Grace glanced up at the antique mirror over the sink. In its reflection, she saw someone who wasn't there: a lithe woman cloistered in a bygone era, wearing a bustle dress and stretching out her arms as if pleading for help.

Grace had seen enough. She frantically sprang to her feet in the bath, but her head struck the shelf against the wall, sending her body ricocheting back into the water. Books tumbled in tandem with her. Along with something else. Grace was underwater when the plugged-in radio submerged, airing a *plunk*.

Sparks shot out, delivering a fatal shock. The water around her erupted in a frenzy of bubbles as the current tore through her, an invisible predator, its fangs embedded deep within muscle and bone. Grace's hefty frame convulsed, her phalanges curling into claws—useless for defense. Cardiac arrest marked the final blow to the introvert.

The radio's sparks faded, becoming a distorted

hum, and the acrid scent of scorched hair pervaded the air. The device, still attached to the socket by its cord, ominously hung suspended in the water's depths, now silent. She floated motionless in a prone position, her scabrous scalp sticking out of the water, resembling an evil island in a sea of acrid tides. Grace Crane existed no more.

★ ★ ★

The next day, rain sullenly rolled into Lafayette, Louisiana, draping the city in a cold, gray curtain. Gloom doggedly clung to every hour, dense as bayou mist. Inside Bernie's Cajun, the air carried a deep, rich scent of black coffee and gumbo, but it was the news that had the joint buzzing.

Flo gruffly said, leaning against the counter and wiping her hands on her apron, "Sheriff heard one of them outta-towners got killed. Bless her heart."

Sheriff Dugas stopped chewing, then swallowed a food mass big enough to fill Lake Michigan. "Yup. Electrocution. Looked tuh be an accident tuh me, ain't no doubt 'bout it." His southern drawl aired as slow as molasses.

Flo's raspy voice asked, "Tell me who done put the radio above the tub?"

"The girls say it come with the house like that."

To the badge, her pale lips airily uttered, "Hmmm."

Flo headed toward a patron, unhurriedly removed

a pencil from behind her ear, and fished an order pad out of her yellow apron.

★ ★ ★

A week had passed since Grace's death. Eleanor and Ann visited a nearby brick library—a quiet sanctuary of brick and mortar, tucked away in a rural corner of town. It seemed like a homey place, the sort of haven where you'd want to curl up in a corner and flip through a Dashiell Hammett novel.

The siblings exchanged simple introductions in the company of a snow-white-haired librarian wearing a gray smock dress, who presented as if she had spent her best years in the past century.

The elderly Louisiana woman cocked her head marginally, studying them with curiosity. "Y'all must be the ladies livin' in that home by the lake." Kindness breathed in the stranger's voice, a softness that hinted at a lifetime of care and consideration toward others.

"How did you know?" replied Ann curiously, her fingers grazing the wooden counter.

"Yer accent, sweetie."

Ann sharply offered an uncomfortable smile.

The librarian slowly resumed, placing two arthritic hands over the desk. "Heard 'bout y'all's kin's passin'. Mighty sorry for your loss."

"Thank you," both sisters said simultaneously.

"I'm surprised," the woman drawled, narrowing her eyes slightly. "Y'all ain't left these parts."

"Why say such a thing?" questioned Eleanor, crossing her arms, airing a hint of umbrage.

"Cause them folks livin' there 'fore y'all just up and packed. Least, that's what we been told."

Eleanor incredulously swiveled her green eyes.

Ann's voice aired as startled. "Do you think something else happened?"

"Dunno. 'Nutha tenant months back was found down in the cellar, hung by a rope. Ruled a suicide."

Ann's face went chalk white. Her torso rigidified; one hand gripped her purse strap.

"Have you lived in Lafayette a while?" Eleanor calmly pressed for information, leaning forward. "Any additional history about the house you recall?"

"All my life, y'know. By now, Mrs. Landry manages it; she's from up north. New York, I think. She met and married Mr. Landry, a local boy, when he was stationed up there in the service." The aged individual paused to catch her breath, then resumed. "Mr. Landry inherited it a few years back by way of his great-aunt Josie's estate. She was Rebecca's younger sister. Lucky for ole Josie, she was stayin' at a friend's place that tragic night in 1885."

The elder exhaled deeply, shaking her head.

"Whoa...who's Rebecca?" asked Ann tremulously.

"What happened in 1885?" interjected Eleanor, unfazed.

"Oh, thought y'knew. Ever'one else does 'round here," the senior citizen said dryly. "I'll 'splain. Mr. Landry's other great-aunt, named Rebecca, barely twenty, stabbed her folks in y'all's residence, utilizing a kitchen knife. It was awful.

"I played in y'all's home as a young'un, used to be real good friends with Rebecca's baby sister, Josie. Mr. Landry's granddaddy, James—their big brother—was off in the Army when it happened. He died young, and the property went to Josie, then to Mr. Landry. His wife runs ever'thin', though."

"What happened to Rebecca?" probed Eleanor, intrigued.

"Died in prison. They say she ain't never uttered another word after her sin."

"Nice story," remarked Ann sarcastically, folding her arms in disgust. "I'm leaving this town tomorrow. And if you're a librarian, why do you keep using the word 'ain't'?"

"Smart for leavin'. I reckon that's just how we all talk 'round here, young lady. Force o' habit, I guess."

"Do you," inquired Eleanor, "store old newspapers here?"

"We harbor copies of *The Lafayette Advertiser* goin' back to 1879. Careful now; they're brittle. But the one y'want's from June 20th, 1885. I keep it in a special spot. Gimme a few minutes."

The librarian disappeared into a private room.

To Eleanor, Ann frankly reiterated, "Tomorrow, I'm hopping on a bus, going back to Indiana."

Eleanor sighed, tucking a stray lock of hair behind her ear and shifting her weight from one foot to the other, impatience simmering in her eyes. "You'll have to take a few to get to Spencer. I'm staying put."

The elder returned and intently laid a discolored newspaper on a shabby table, smoothing it out with careful hands. After she did, her voice warned, "There ain't no peace in that house. See the headline? Folks 'round here still call it Blood Mansion."

* * *

Eleanor's pencil, possessing a mind of its own, eerily waltzed along the page as if guided by an unseen hand. The bay window's alcove had become her dust-ridden sanctuary; a tiny desk buried under scattered pages, the wastebasket beside it overflowing with abandoned attempts. Spirits were among her, she felt sure of it. They whispered, coaxing her writing instrument, creating a silent partnership.

Midnight hunger's gnawing grip and unease sent Ann downstairs for a snack. Descending the creaking staircase, Ann and her trailing silhouette stealthily made their way to the dimly lit kitchen. Eleanor, still journaling, remained too preoccupied to spare her sibling a glance.

To herself, Ann bitterly muttered, "How can she be so oblivious to what's happening here?"

Ann finished the peanut butter and jelly sandwich, then ascended the steps. A half-full glass of milk was still in her right hand. At the top, her gaze rapidly flicked to a tarnished mirror across the hall.

A ghastly male figure materialized in the reflection where no man should be. His handlebar mustache curled at its edges. A frock coat was draped over narrow shoulders, and a bowler hat projected a shadow upon hollow eyes.

The apparition's mouth hung open in an inaudible wail. Ann's breath shuddered. In the mirror, the specter desperately reached toward her, fingers outstretched, seeking solace.

"Aaaahhh!" she screamed in panic, her limbs stiffening with terror.

For a few seconds, Ann stood in a torpid state, but she lost her footing on the runner carpet. She toppled down the steps behind her, rolling in an unsettling disarray.

The tumbler of milk violently shattered against the railing. White liquid spattered, bearing resemblance to a sneeze, sailing toward the first floor.

Startled, Eleanor urgently rushed up the staircase, her respirations erratically quickening. She froze mid-step, then instinctively cowered when she encountered Ann's still body, mimicking a discarded ragdoll. Her sister was lying supine transversely on the half landing, where the stairs twisted like a cruel, unforgiving turn in one labyrinth of the forsaken house.

★   ★   ★

One day later in a barren hospital room, fat Sheriff Dugas, thick-necked and sweating, loomed at Ann's bedside, heavy boots scuffing black streaks on the cracked tile. She was sitting up, her left arm in a white cast.

"'Preciate the tale, ma'am, one hella one," he grunted hoarsely, deliberately folding two pudgy arms across a flabby chest. "Ain't no way I'm slappin' charges on a ghost, but I'll tell yuh this: you best bolt outta that house while yuh still can. The place is downright haunted."

Ann swallowed hard, a chill creeping through the marrow of her spine. Before she could speak, Eleanor gingerly entered from the hallway. Sheriff Dugas tipped his hat respectfully, his expression unreadable.

"Howdy, ma'am," he muttered.

To Ann, he said curtly, egressing the scene, "You best take care now."

"What'd he want?" asked Eleanor, perching over Ann awkwardly.

"Simply wanted to know how I ended up here," she replied softly, omitting the lawman's theoretical warning.

"How are you feeling?"

"Okay, not so punchy." She shifted uncomfortably

in her bed. "They say I'm lucky, I suffered only a concussion and a fractured arm."

"Sorry this happened."

"Eleanor, a phantom in the mirror was reaching out at me."

"I believe you. I sense their presence."

Ann's eyes reflected the vicissitudes of their Louisiana excursion, revealing the growing distance between her and Eleanor. "Once I'm released tomorrow, bring me straight to the bus station."

"Okay."

Ann intently studied Eleanor's stoic façade. "So, you're not returning to Indiana?"

"Nope. I leased it for a year, paid upfront. No refunds. Remember?"

The next day, in her old heap, Eleanor drove Ann from the hospital to the bus station, broadcasting a face akin to a marble statue.

At the terminal, a gray-haired driver laboriously hoisted Ann's battered suitcase onboard, and the sisters traded stilted goodbyes—Eleanor all frost, Ann all nerves. She boarded the Greyhound heading north, settling into the third seat, eyes straight ahead.

Nearby, tucked within the shadows of a smoky café, Mrs. Landry lurked, purposefully hidden behind an extra-wide-brimmed hat and dark shades, spying. Her countenance cast a speckle of malice as she stirred a hot beverage in a slow, deliberate motion. Her lips cruelly curled into a faint, scornful smile.

★   ★   ★

Two more days passed. Another slow, dragging day at Bernie's Cajun, where time moved as sluggishly as a lone bayou turtle shell wafting aimlessly through marshy waters. Mrs. Landry perched stiffly on a stool, smoke eddying languidly above her Bakelite cigarette holder like a lazy fog. Meanwhile, Flo's bare cig dangled from her lips, free of such an ostentatious accessory.

In the far corner Sheriff Dugas, his gut spilling over his belt, loomed in what locals called "Duggie's throne," puffing smoke analogous to a locomotive bound for nowhere. By virtue of his badge, he held court over a kingdom of bottom-shelf bourbon disciples.

Eleanor Crane stepped in hesitantly, draped in dime-store threads doing her no favors. She made her way to Mrs. Landry.

"I need," Eleanor requested of Landry, "all the mirrors removed in that house."

"Thought you fancied ghosts," snickered the lavish woman in the soft lavender floral-print dress, the delicate ruffle at its neckline framing her face as she sipped a cup of coffee. The dress had a cinched waist, and a hemline which terminated just below the knees. The wide-brimmed hat rested beside her on the table.

"For my writing I need to feel them, not see them."

"I'll send for Felix." Mrs. Landry delivered an exaggerated eye roll in Flo's direction.

An hour passed, the sun hanging low, mirroring a rotting orange in the sky. One hundred feet distal to the house by the lake, Felix emerged out of the brush garbed in his usual fishing attire. He plodded along the gravel driveway, hauling a large duffel bag that weighed him down like a sinus infection.

Across the road, Sheriff Dugas eyed the scene shrewdly, peering out the dirty window of the diner, his eyes sharp as a hawk's, his meaty buttocks glued to a stool as if they had been cursed.

The moment Felix vanished from view, Dugas's hind parted from the padded seat grudgingly, then rose.

Felix employed oversized, bony knuckles to produce three knocks on the archaic wooden door.

Eleanor warily opened the door. Felix lingered in the threshold, his spine exhibiting a bizarre, contorted posture. Five words came out of his oral cavity, echoing a slow poison. "I told ya to leeeeave."

The ghost writer stared at him, showcasing pity, and curtly urged, "Please take down the mirrors, Felix." She led him into the house.

"Yes, ma'am." He followed.

Eleanor heard the bag of tools clunk on the floor before the cold steel pipe wrench impetuously clocked her posterior skull. It was the last sound she'd ever hear. Darkness swallowed her whole.

The front door hung ajar until the sheriff kicked it fully open. Felix impassively stood over his victim, carrying the deadly plumbing tool in one hand.

Killer and lawman locked eyes unflinchingly, the silence between them dense as graveyard fog.

"Felix," Sheriff Dugas drawled, coated in an air of nonchalance, "yuh done good, son. Feed her to them gators. Sink that car in the swamp. I'll tell yer PO you're workin' out well round here."

Beyond Dugas, just outside the threshold, Mrs. Landry extended an arm and impertinently beckoned two polished fingers at Felix. He obeyed, moving toward her.

She extended a palm in a stop motion, then ordered, "Felix, go fetch what I asked for."

Felix withdrew obediently from the foyer and climbed the interior stairwell. Ninety seconds later, he reemerged dutifully outside, pressing a thick roll of greenbacks atop her waiting hand.

Rotating her wrist, Landry halved the stack— one portion slipped into her handbag, the other she split again, Sheriff Dugas claiming the bulk. Felix received what was left. The authority figure's double chin nodded in assent. The creep stuffed his paltry portion in his fishing vest, void of negation.

"Got two payouts on this one," imparted Mrs. Landry. "The dame played hard to get rid of."

The crooked officer tipped his big hat, expressing gallantry. "Glad t'be of 'ssistance, Mrs. Landry."

To Felix, Mrs. Landry sharply chided, "Clean that bloody mess up, every bit of it, and leave those mirrors alone."

"Yes, ma'am. What 'bout this here?" He held up a bundle of typewritten pages, bound together loosely with twine.

Wicked Mrs. Landry snatched and examined it. Following the perusal, she murmured, "Good find, Felix. Eleanor's manuscript...*Blood Mansion.*"

To Dugas, she said, "Maybe three payouts. I'll put my name on it, then submit to some publishing companies. We'll split the profit like a pie." The devilish woman chuckled smugly and added, "Of course, give Felix the smaller slice."

"Lookin' forward," Dugas effused, "to doin' more business with yuh, Mrs. Landry. Sure glad yuh done made our town yer own. Specially with yuh bein' a Yankee an' all."

She smirked. "Yes, now let us shift our attention to finding the next potential fleece; hopefully, another wayfarer." Landry's tone was serious, to the point.

The two men in the femme fatale's audience nodded.

The sinister cabal broke up. Dugas's boots crunched on the gravel, and Mrs. Landry slipped gracefully behind the wheel of her Lincoln, bidding no further words.

Nightfall found Felix finishing his twisted chores, saving the simplest for the encore. Using a steady hand, he drove a stake into the earth—the *For Rent* sign was reborn.

⋆ ⋆ ⋆

Miles away, Ann's final bus approached Spencer, Indiana. Mrs. Landry's words, "They won't hurt you," replayed in her head. Ann gazed out the window wistfully, her breath fogging the glass, wondering if she'd ever lay eyes on Eleanor again.

Only three souls in this world knew the answer to that rumination.

7

BUS DRIVER

September '47. On a dreary evening in Ohio, dusk began creeping in. On a corner in Cincinnati's Price Hill district, a transit vehicle hissed to a stop, its headlights slicing faint, hazy streaks through the downpour. One bus driver gave a friendly wave to another, acknowledging the free lift.

Józef Wozniak, clad in work attire, exited the city bus that carried him home every night. At five foot eleven, the fortyish man had a broad torso and a sturdy build, though a soft belly pressed against his damp uniform shirt. Never one for umbrellas, he let the drizzle bead on his cap, which rested low over his brow, hiding straggly blonde hair. Shoulders ached from twelve hours behind the wheel. Hooded, blood-shot eyes pointed low, staring at neon reflections cast by illuminations above, shimmering in the puddles.

It wasn't a good moment to ascend the stairs to

his third-floor apartment; maybe it never was. Mr. Wozniak knew an increased probability existed that he would run into the man who made his nerves brittle—the one Cincy newspapers called Moondog Malkasian, a known associate of the city's underworld, who lurked too often in the second-floor hallway.

An acrid stench of stale cigarettes lingered in the air as Mr. Wozniak wearily climbed the creaking steps, leaving a trail of rainwater in his wake. A raucous noise—constant banging—grew louder with each rise. When he reached the second-floor landing, his stomach coiled. He gripped the railing, pulse thudding in his ears. The thumping intensified. A short, rugged fellow, rocked forward and back on his feet, his forehead smacking the wall brutally, like a broken machine.

In the corridor beside the nutcase, affixed to the wall, was a shared community phone that served both the second- and third-floor residents. The device itself, a relic having its origin in the previous decade, consisted of a separate earpiece and mouthpiece—the kind that required an operator to place a call. Mr. Wozniak fancied it for one reason: free service. What he didn't fancy was the dwelling's sociopath, who always loitered nearby.

Mr. Wozniak furtively tiptoed toward the third-floor staircase set back off the landing—a transient sanctuary from Moondog.

He damn near touched it when the banging

ceased. A familiar, hectoring utterance cut through the hallway—"What yuh lookin' at, Polack?"

"Wasn't looking," countered Wozniak, delicately opening a palm while shifting his weight back a step.

The squat man owning a cursed visage barreled across the cracked linoleum, encroaching on the bus driver's personal space. His strides were choppy but urgent, the speed unsettling. Predatory black orbits sat beneath abundant, unruly hair, and his tan, scarred kisser was etched with something mean; he might have shaved two days ago. A white undershirt plus dungarees hung off his stocky, iron frame.

Moondog Malkasian peered up, his gruff voice rumbling guttural and fierce in gravelly thunder, as if mocking the world in blithe indifference.

"Huh?" His hot breath burned against Wozniak's cheek.

"I wasn't looking at you, sir," the Polish immigrant reiterated, this time pitching a higher degree of politeness.

Satisfied by his intimidation tactic, Mr. Malkasian sneered. "Hey, can yuh figure out women?" He scratched at a flake of dried skin near his temple—peepers glinting.

"They're a difficult species," Mr. Wozniak replied, unsure if the words even made sense. Anything to placate the crazy man.

The phone in the hall rang. Without a second

thought, Mr. Malkasian darted toward it, as if answering an impromptu summons sent by fate.

Whew, Mr. Wozniak mused. A fugacious sense of safety washed over him as he crested the final flight, relieved his weary bones had survived another day, though he comprehended that tomorrow might not be so kind.

Muffled yelling echoed from below, then faded in a slow diminuendo as he elevated higher. He knew, deep down, he had to get out of this apartment building. Saving up acted as the catalyst for him clocking extra hours and the reason Wanda, his wife, recently picked up a job at Hudepohl Brewery.

Józef Wozniak landed in the States after leaving Warsaw when he was five, gradually shedding his Polish accent as he Americanized. Wanda, arriving at eighteen, still carried her native tongue in every conversation.

He unlocked the wooden door to apartment 3A, a dingy, cramped, three-room tenement. In the kitchen, Wanda and a refrigerated bottle of Hudepohl Lager were waiting for him.

Wanda was thirty-five, a woman of sturdy build, shaped by arduous labor but never stripped of her femininity. Her round face, neither too gentle nor severe, bore high Slavic cheekbones, plus a straight, practical nose. Hazel eyes, shifting between brown and green with the light, held a quiet intensity; an expression of someone who had seen hardship but chose not to dwell on it. Dark lashes framed those watchful pupils, her slightly arched brows lending an air of righteous authority.

Her voluminous, light brown hair was neatly braided and pinned at the nape of her neck, a few stubborn strands curling alongside prominent temples. Strong hands, forged by kneading dough, bore the visible proof of cultural toil. She wore a simple, practical green dress and flat-heeled shoes, clothing intended for purpose rather than vanity.

Józef spoke first, his tone heavy, bearing urgency. "Honey, we have to find a better place. If I say the wrong thing, that lunatic downstairs is going to explode."

"We have," Wanda disclosed, studying his wetness from crown to toe, "more big troubles." She handed him the beer.

"Eh?"

She called her son. "Stanislaw, come here now, yeh?" She glanced toward the hallway, jaw set firm.

"Please refer to him as Stanley, Wanda; this is America."

Eleven-year-old Stanley, a husky boy for his age, sullenly emerged from a bedroom, his bushy blonde hair tousled, holding a makeshift ice pack to his swollen lip.

★   ★   ★

In his work uniform, Józef Wozniak stood dourly at the brick elementary school's front entrance, taking in the worn, yet steadfast structure. The building loomed large against the gray skies of Cincinnati, its redbrick walls etched with decades of history. The city's industrial air pervaded his nasal cavity like a venomous toxin.

Weathered windows cast their gaze over the concrete schoolyard where children would normally rush to play, but today the area presented as oddly distant and empty. Mr. Wozniak had trodden these same grounds as a boy. The institution had changed little, but the weight of his son's troubles made it feel foreign now.

Wozniak's hands trembled slightly, a mix of frustration and helplessness tightening in his chest. A burdensome devoir he could neither escape nor fulfill.

Inside, the principal's office appeared unwelcoming, its polished oak desk catching the harsh glare of fluorescent lights. The headmaster, Mr. Hamilton, a portly, bald chap in a tan suit, sat behind it, carrying an air of indifference suggesting tacitly a bus driver existed beneath him on the word's hierarchy.

Hamilton's oval spectacles perched low on his nose as he leafed through papers. Fatty's expansive butterfly ears looked as though they might carry his corpulent head into aerial flight if his formidable frame weren't anchored to it.

The room reeked of cigar residue, and his voice, when he finally spoke, sounded flat and uninterested.

"So, your boy's being bullied?" Barely glancing up from the paperwork, Mr. Hamilton continued, "Not our problem. It's not as if it happened here, on our grounds." He shrugged a shoulder dismissively, seemingly treating it as some small matter, no more important than a can of beans. "You know how kids are, Mr. Wozniak. They fight, they tease, they forget."

An aggrieved Mr. Wozniak's jaw clenched as the sweat pores on his neck opened up in a trickle, his skin prickling with raw tension. An image of Stanley, pulverized by the other boys on the way home, flooded his mind. The transit driver's fists balled at his sides, but he forced himself to stay calm. He wasn't here to start a fight; however, the anger burned in him nonetheless.

"I don't care if it's off school property," Mr. Wozniak decisively uttered, pointing a thick finger. His tone was ironclad, a storm brewing internally. "Those boys attend class here, and they're hurting my son. It's your responsibility to stop it."

The snob's rotund phiz remained impassive; not a minuscule hint of empathy glimmered in his eyes.

Hamilton adjusted his cuffs, slow and methodical. "Well, we can't be responsible for everything, Mr. Wozniak. School hours are one thing, but other than that, we can't do much," he said, his words hanging in the air, contemptuous and cold, waving a hand as if swatting away an insignificant demerit on a student's record.

Mr. Wozniak departed the dismal office, feeling smaller than he had when he entered, his heart sinking deeper, step by step. Presently, the city outside seemed more oppressive, its weight pressing down on both shoulders. How was he supposed to protect his son if those meant to ensure his safety turned their backs on him?

The sound of the door closing behind him reverberated in the hall, as if it had slammed shut on a father's faith in humanity.

* * *

A day later, Moondog Malkasian edgily slouched against the doorframe of his threadbare apartment, the glow of his cigarette carving a lonely ember in the dim hallway. Smoke languidly coiled around him as he desperately waited for a telephone call which would never come.

Was it from a frightened dame who'd already skipped town? Or was the old phone merely toying with him, stretching the silence until he snapped? Only a sane individual could astutely decipher the difference.

The explosive man watched little Stanley stumble onto the second-floor landing, clutching his bloody nose, hands trembling. The lad fearfully gazed up, eyes wide, and for an instant, Moondog saw something fragile in him. Something akin to his younger self.

"Again? Yuh ain't gonna let 'em push yuh 'round like this, huh, kid?" Moondog growled, his voice rough, coated in grit. The floor below groaned as he aggressively approached Stanley.

An abashed Stanley froze, then lowered his gaze. Malkasian's words made his stomach twist—intestines knotting themselves in pure humiliation.

The syndicate enforcer cracked his knuckles and venomously peered low. "Ain't 'bout what they did to yuh, pal. It's 'bout what yer old man never taught yuh."

Placing a calloused hand on Stanley's left shoulder, the uncivilized Armenian pulled him forward, the weight of his grip analogous to a duffel bag filled with rocks.

"C'mon, kid. Imma show yuh how tuh fight yer own battles."

Moondog clamped a hand on the kid's shoulder and steered him hard down the stairs, his grasp unyielding. Stanley's breath came in frantic bursts, but his terrified feet kept moving—Moondog wouldn't approve of terrified.

It was something—anything—better than the abuse he'd endured fifteen minutes ago. Soon Stanley found himself being hauled past the basement entrance, deeper into a shadowed stairwell, heading toward a place destined to change the lives of two lone wolves forever.

⋆   ⋆   ⋆

The next afternoon, Stanley stood on the exact cracked sidewalk where the three bullies usually cornered him, his hands sweating, but his heart steadier than before. Today, he didn't rush home.

He spotted the trio of juveniles swaggering his way, sneers already forming on their faces, mirroring old scars. Even though Stanley was larger than any of the punks, they closed in, confidently ready to push him around, as they always did.

However, Stanley wasn't the same kid anymore. He recalled the resonance of Moondog's vicious two-hour lesson—the way he had drilled him over and over: *Keep yer stance firm, hit hard, show no fear.*

A freckle-faced boy, the gang's leader, smirked beneath an askew ball cap, wearing a gabardine windbreaker and too-short trousers, then lunged forward.

Stanley positioned himself, rooted, bent an elbow, then, in a swift, clean motion, as instructed, delivered an open-hand chop to the youth's nose, employing the ulnar edge of his palm.

The jolt of impact on Stanley's opponent's facial bone traveled through the air, and the bully staggered hindward, wrenching his lip in agony, then began to cry.

For a moment, the two spectators remained paralyzed, awestruck. Suddenly, without a word, they scattered, mimicking cockroaches in the light, their bravado dissolving into surrender.

Stanley lingered, statuesque, mirth curling on his lips, buoyant as he realized he wasn't a victim anymore.

★   ★   ★

To the man at the table, the cramped kitchen felt suffocating, a flickering bulb above casting a feeble, wavering light. Mr. Wozniak, still in his work clothes, slumped opposite a half-eaten plate of pierogi, his paw-like hands clutching a bottle of Hudepohl Lager.

Wanda, dressed demurely in a plaid cotton dress, stood at the sink scrubbing an enamelware pot with more force than necessary, muscles tensing, fingers gripping the handle tightly, a frown tugging at her lips. Scalding water surged over the rim, soaking her apron.

"Stanislaw should be here," she muttered grimly over her shoulder, her Polish accent rich, rolling syllables as if they carried the weight of old country winters.

"He's teaching him how to fight, Wanda," Mr. Wozniak countered, his voice low—almost grateful. "This Moondog, he's doing what no one else would. Our son...he's got no courage. Stanley can't keep getting picked on. It made me proud that he scared off three bullies yesterday."

Wanda pivoted sharply, her hazel eyes flashing fiercely. The pot clanged in the sink, a cymbal crash.

"You don't understand, Józef. Dis Moondog...he's no good. I hear tings. The Outfit, you know? He breaks legs for dem, collects debts. You tink it's safe for our Stanislaw to be around him?" Her voice grew tight, laced with worry. "Moondog's dangerous, Józef. Dese men, dey kill people."

He slipped an objection in contrarily. "Stanley's not gonna kill anyone, the man's just coaching him." Mr. Wozniak sighed, leaning rearward in his chair.

"No!" Wanda snapped curtly, shaking her head slowly, resolutely. "Our boy requires a fah-ther, not some gangster! I won't have him transformed into one of dem. You've been ter-ree-fied of dis man since we rented dis dump. Dis Moondog, he's poison, and it'll seep into Stanislaw's bones. Mark my words, Józef, it's unsafe, all of it."

Wanda's lecture sealed Mr. Wozniak's mouth, his thoughts clouding as he wondered if he was protecting his son...or merely letting the darkness creep in.

Wanda's entreaty was incisive, her desperate eyes pleading. "Go check on our boy down in dat basement, huh?"

"Not tonight, dear, not tonight."

⋆   ⋆   ⋆

Two days later, Mr. Wozniak had been summoned back to Principal Hamilton's gloomy office. The atmosphere had shifted; however, not in a way which pleased the headmaster. The same unforgiving fluorescent lights cast their harsh glow over the imposing, polished oak desk, but this time, Mr. Hamilton's prior air of disinterest was tinged noticeably with irritation. Fingers drummed restlessly upon the wood, his giant-sized ears twitched. He removed his glasses, pinching the bridge of his nose before leveling a morose mask of forced patience at Mr. Wozniak.

"It seems we've developed an urgent new issue, Mr. Wozniak," Hamilton divulged, voice stern. "Your son has taken to—shall we say—turning the tables? We've had indignant parental complaints. I cannot have students behaving like brash street fighters. Violence," he declared, spreading his hands as if he were some great arbiter of justice, "is unacceptable."

Mr. Wozniak kept his expression neutral, though inside, a smirk unfurled in the recesses of his mind, fancying the reverse of the coin. The bus driver folded his arms, letting the silence stretch, purposely causing Hamilton to fidget.

"So, let me grasp it straight," he finally said, tone prolonged, deliberate. "When my son was getting beaten, that wasn't the school's problem? But now, seeing he's defending himself, suddenly, it is?"

The hypocrisy left him astounded.

"I'm simply asserting there needs to be order, Mr. Wozniak. And it starts with Stanley recognizing his proper place."

A flicker of something satisfying passed through Mr. Wozniak's eyes. He slanted forward barely, his voice quiet but steel-edged. "Oh, he comprehends his new place." The father rose, straightening his uniform shirt at the waist via a sharp tug. "And it's not on the ground."

Making his point, Wozniak egressed, leaving the burly, bald Hamilton fuming behind his desk, the scent of stale tobacco billowing like an old, losing argument.

*   *   *

That evening, following Wanda's reinforced orders, Mr. Wozniak descended to the first floor, hesitating warily for a few seconds at the top of the basement stairs. The air underneath him seemed thick with mildew and something worse. Something curdled in his gut. The chain of a hulking bag squeaked below; a metronome of violence, immutable, unabated. His fingers gripped the rail as he took an initial step into the depths, black work shoes scuffing along worn wood.

This was the area of the apartment building where others didn't dare venture—a domain besides the hallway where Moondog Malkasian lurked.

A floor lower, his son Stanley's meaty fists hammered a dense bag relentlessly, leather slamming against leather, filling the dank, low-lit basement. Perspiration poured down the youth's face, his knuckles

raw. Moondog Malkasian loomed over him, crookedly grinning, a devil in the shadows, understanding the boy was getting deadlier by the day, each strike coming harder than the last, a fuse burning shorter.

"That's it, kid," Moondog growled coarsely, eyes narrowed, watching Stanley's every move. "Yuh ain't gonna be nobody's spittoon no more. Yuh keep hit 'em like yuh mean it. Punch wit' fury. Punch wit' all yuh got. The bag's one of dem punks who been messin' wit' yuh."

The rugged eleven-year-old, wearing indigo-blue dungarees plus a white undershirt, ruthlessly punched and punched again. Then he retreated rearward, panting, his face set in pugnacious determination.

"I did it, Mr. Malkasian," imparted Stanley, his voice rougher now, more confident. "Two more of 'em today. Beat 'em down, just as you taught me."

Moondog chuckled darkly, leaning against a grimy cement wall, flaunting his crossed, tattooed arms.

"That's what I like tuh hear, kid. You're gettin' good at it. Yuh beat 'em tuh the ground, yeah? Showed 'em who's boss?" His lips curled into a cruel smile. "Yuh keep winnin', ain't no bully gonna look at yuh sideways. Yuh ain't no bum no more. Yer-uh a goddamn beast. Make 'em fear yuh."

Stanley nodded, his fists clenched, his skeleton shaking with a surge of adrenaline. There was no turning back. The more he fought, the more he desired it.

Mr. Wozniak reached the bottom step, hearing it all. He saw barbells and dumbbells rolled out across the floor, exactly as his son had mentioned. In his mind, he revisited Stanley's actions last evening—flexing biceps, exclaiming, "Dad, Dad, I'm lifting weights!"

Through the dimness, Moondog jolted upright and advanced toward Mr. Wozniak, crowding the man's space, his two eyes gleaming—similar to a predator sizing up its prey—his grin stretching into something malevolent.

"Thanks for helping Stanley, sir. He's much stronger. Do I call you Moondog?" the father muttered, his voice taut, his belly twisting with unease.

The leg breaker chuckled, low and dangerous. "You don't know me well enough tuh be throwin' names like dat. Yeah, kid's stronguh. But yuh made 'em weak. Soft."

He menacingly edged nearer, the air around them thickening. "Kid must learn tuh survive. Ain't no room fuh wimps in this jungle. Yuh think yuh can keep 'em safe, but all yuh did wuz paint a target on his ass."

Moondog paused, his gaze hardening by the second.

"I owe," Mr. Wozniak promised, extending his arm for a handshake, "you a favor."

"You do owe me, Polack. Yer-uh gonna pay up, one way or another." The enforcer declined Wozniak's meeting of the palms gesture and asked, "Yer-uh a bus drivuh huh?"

★   ★   ★

The next evening, Józef Wozniak trudged wearily up the stairs, hauling very little on his mind besides Wanda's cooking. On his ascent, he listlessly studied the holes in the wall's cracked horsehair plaster and comically thought, *No doubt, Moondog's doing.*

He barely made it to the second-floor landing before stopping short, as the dry humor was abruptly expelled from his body, akin to a cartoon character running away from a haunted house.

A man perched on the top step, legs leisurely stretched yonder, as if to reveal he wasn't moving unless he decided to. He sported a black suit, no hat, no cigarette, a thin sneer, and a zany haircut that had no business outside the center of a bandstand. Mr. Wozniak instantly recognized him, courtesy of prior union meetings. Cincy newspapers dubbed him Petey Pompadour, a pizza-faced racketeer with a thin mustache, as unwelcoming as the city's back alleys.

But, unlike Moondog Malkasian, who carried all muscle and no brain, Petey owned a countenance that spoke in debts and ordered executions. The fellow was a bona fide member of the Cincinnati Outfit. Paradoxically, Moondog only served as an expendable accessory.

Wozniak gasped raggedly. His nerves prickled, like

he'd plunged into a frigid draft, hoping that coiffure wasn't here for him. *He's here to visit Moondog, that's it.*

Disturbingly, he perceived Moondog Malkasian circling the platform, resembling a caged beast, muttering, twitching, a one-man parade to nowhere. The stubby, thick lug pummeled his chest, then unleashed a howl that rattled down all the way to hell.

Petey Pompadour ignored Moondog's insane antics. He had other business on this stairwell. The fop lifted a hand, palm outward, stalling Wozniak in his tracks.

"Hold it, Polack." Petey's tone seemed polished—a gentlemanly blade, smooth enough to sell a lemon to a carnivore. Beneath it all, there existed asperity, a calloused edge that rasped, echoing sandpaper over steel.

Józef Wozniak froze three steps below the landing, his heartbeat a little too fast for comfort. He reckoned it was time to settle on the unwanted obligation. Feeling the compression of his ribs, the Polish-American's breath came slow, but his voice aired steady. "What do you need from me?" he asked solemnly. "I'm grateful for Mr. Malkasian coaching my son."

"If you owe Moondog a favor, then you owe us a favor," Petey said, casual as a butcher sizing up a cut of meat.

The gangster slanted forward, resting one elbow on his knee, eyes jagged like broken glass in a gutter, staring at Wozniak's uniform as if sizing up whether this dupe possessed the temerity to refuse.

"You're a bus driver. How convenient. We require somebody transported. A witness...one we don't dig. You won't have to get your hands dirty." He let the words linger, allowing Wozniak to fill in the blanks. Then Petey smiled, a thin, humorless smirk, and flatly added "Do the deed, and we're even."

*   *   *

The day of reckoning had arrived for Mr. Wozniak. Downtown Cincinnati, Fountain Square, the cool air sat heavy in his lungs. Petey Pompadour, donned in a cranberry-colored suit, briskly popped the trunk of an Oldsmobile. Inside, another transit driver lay haphazardly bound and gagged, his uniform rumpled, eyes pleading.

Mr. Wozniak's breath faltered. His stomach grew sour. His fingers twitched at his hips.

"Don't worry," Petey lazily drawled, rolling a toothpick between his teeth. "We'll let your chum go once the job's done."

Mr. Wozniak swallowed deep. "Okay-okay, please, he's-he's got a family." His voice hoarsely cracked on the last word.

Without a blink, the mobster slammed the trunk shut with a finality that rattled Wozniak's bones, then motioned him toward the front of the black Cadillac. Petey didn't walk—he sauntered like trouble in expensive clothes. A street map unfurled over the hood, creased and smudged.

"You know ole Tons of Rope's route?" asked Petey sardonically.

Wozniak licked his dry lips. "N-not really."

"Learn it!"

Mr. Wozniak stared at Petey's layout, his mind racing for a way out. But every angle he considered led to the same bleak conclusion: he was stymied. No escape, no refusal, not unless he wanted to put his own family in danger.

Petey stabbed a finger at the map. "You're driving the West 9th Street bus outta the city. Follow?" He jabbed it again, further left, where a big X had been written in pencil. "You pick up Moondog here—before our little witness gets off. It's a bogus stop. Follow?"

Wozniak nodded quickly. "Uh-huh. Moondog at the X." His pulse pounded in his ears.

Petey's voice stayed nonchalant, as if he were giving directions to a picnic. "After that, it's only the witness and Moondog onboard. The last stop's supposed to be the snitch's, but you're not braking there." He insistently tapped the map once more. "You continue past the West 8th Street Bridge. Moondog'll handle the rest," Petey instructed, his voice slick with the casual turpitude of a man who arranged death sentences as easily as dinner reservations.

The syndicate member went on, "He'll take care

of biz, then haul Snitchy's corpse off the bus and plunge it in the drink. Goodbye squawk box. See?"

Wozniak felt sweat beads accumulating at his temples.

Petey coolly resumed, "Oh, and flip the sign—'Out of Service.' No new passengers. Just you, the witness, and good ol' Moondog. Follow?"

Wozniak's head bobbed like a marionette's. "G-got it." His hands clenched, fists caging the tremors.

Petey deviously grinned. "Good boy."

The words slithered into Mr. Wozniak's entrails, cold as the Ohio River.

★ ★ ★

Dusk set in on Cincinnati. The bus heavily lumbered along, shedding passengers at each corner. With the "Out of Service" sign flipped in its frame, no new riders boarded. A few tried, but Mr. Wozniak waved them away, employing a nervous flick of his wrist.

Rolling toward the inner city's edge, he snatched a glance in the rearview. One passenger remained: a stone-faced fella in a sharp blue suit, buried in a newspaper. Wozniak bit his inner lip. *Poor bastard*, he mused, squeezing the wheel tighter. *But it's him or me.*

Moondog would be waiting at that phony stop soon. Wozniak could almost taste the end of this rotten day.

Then, unheralded, the man in the suit rose and strode smoothly forward. A rough hand clamped down on Wozniak's shoulder, fingers digging like iron bolts.

"Pull ovuh. Right here." His voice sounded low, grave. "You see Moondog, don't ya?"

A bead of sweat formed on Wozniak's temple. "I—uh—figured you were the witness."

"Nah. Name's Sammy. We ain't about to trust you on your own, pal."

Mr. Wozniak pondered uneasily. *What? Alone? Are they coming for me? Did they think I was a witness to something?*

"Cut the juice," the gangster called Sammy ordered superciliously.

Out the windshield, Moondog was approaching the curb, eyes feral, a switchblade gleaming in his grip.

Mr. Wozniak applied the brakes. Sammy yanked the release lever, popping the door before the Outfit's dupe hatched any brave ideas.

Wozniak rotated his cranium all around.

The racketeer leaned in close. His breath smelled of something awful. "She's curled up, readin' a book. Window seat near the back, dummy."

A shiver ran down Wozniak's vertebral column. His mind spun. *The dame, the one in the flowered hat. The pretty one. Dark skin.* He never saw her get off. *They wouldn't kill a woman. Would they?*

Moondog stomped up the steps, his weapon still in hand. "Keep drivin', Polack," he sneered, standing over the transit driver. "The bridge, remembuh?"

Wozniak's chin tightened. He hated the "P" word. "You didn't mention the witness was a she," he contested, though his voice lacked conviction.

Moondog's lip twisted. "Drive."

Twenty-five feet away, the woman untangled herself, sensing something wasn't quite right. She rose cautiously, her wary eyes darting between the men. Moondog and Sammy advanced toward her, closing the space between them.

Something lionhearted ignited in Wozniak. He jerked the wheel and stomped the gas abruptly, scaling the curb. The bus bucked, lurching wildly, bearing resemblance to a wild boar. The woman tumbled onto a seat, while Moondog and Sammy clung to the rails to stay upright. Automobile horns blared, and heads on the sidewalk pivoted.

The moment the vehicle halted, Wozniak jumped into action. From the rear, he hurled himself at Moondog, hitting him hard. They crashed to the floor, the knife skittering under a seat. Sammy lunged forward at the witness. The woman reached for something— her purse, no?—something inside it.

Wozniak dug his knees into Moondog's spine, pressing, utilizing every ounce of strength he had. To the unknown passenger, he shouted vehemently, "Run! Your life's in danger!"

"I knew this day would come!" she exclaimed, her face drawing taut with dread.

Sammy grabbed a fistful of her hair.

The woman deftly rotated her arm over Sammy's shoulder, and his eyes went wide. An ice pick jutted grotesquely from his skull.

She didn't hesitate. She ripped it out and drove it home again. And again. And again.

Meanwhile, Moondog thrashed ferociously beneath his temporary captor.

"Run!" Wozniak bellowed. "Run!"

The so-called witness exited the rear door, fleeing. Her screams sliced through the air as she barreled frantically along a pavement engulfed by the darkness.

Moondog exploded free, turning on Wozniak with fists like sledgehammers. A left to the ribs. A right to the jaw. The driver's head snapped back, vision waning dizzily. An additional blow sent him sprawling into the fare box.

Before Moondog could finish the job, two bluecoats stormed the bus, guns drawn, voices barking. They piled onto him, wrestling him down, pinning his arms behind his torso.

Moondog Malkasian was off the streets, and a corpse once known as Sammy necessitated transport to the morgue.

*   *   *

A day passed. In their cubby bedroom, Józef and Wanda Wozniak filled their suitcases in a frantic, clumsy rhythm, as if time were of the essence. They moved fast—slow meant danger.

In another room, a *Cincinnati Enquirer* lay sprawled open on the kitchen table, its bold headlines blaring the latest scandal:

SAMMY RUSSO SLAIN!
KIDNAPPED BUS DRIVER FOUND ALIVE!
SECOND DRIVER CLEARED OF WRONGDOING
JEWELRY STORE HEIST WITNESS SECURED IN
POLICE PROTECTION
PETEY POMPADOUR SKIPPED TOWN
MOONDOG MALKASIAN BOOKED FOR
ATTEMPTED MURDER

The ink still looked fresh, but to the couple packing, the story was already fading into the past replaced by the more pressing necessity of escape.

"Imagine the detective telling me not to leave town. Needs my testimony against that lunatic," Józef Wozniak scoffed cynically.

"Nie, Józef, you cannot take," said Wanda, bearing down on the suitcase lid, applying two adamant hands, "de stand against Moondog. Is suicide!"

"Yeah, I can see him doing circles in his cell as we speak."

"Bein' charged for attempted murder and kidnappin'? You are number one on his mind now, yes?"

"Yes, let testifying be the female witness's problem."

She nodded in agreement, straightened her posture, and locked her luggage. "Where is Stanisław?"

Józef shut his case with a snap. "Wanda, wherever we end up, please—address him as Stanley."

"Nie, you are not," she uttered steadfastly, "makin' de rules nie more."

In the basement, Stanley hammered the punching bag, wielding fists of anger. Moondog Malkasian's truculent words played repeatedly in his head—*Keep your stance firm, hit hard, show no fear. Punch wit fury. Punch wit all yuh got.*

8

BREAD BASKET

September '47, 7 p.m.. On a gloomy evening in Baltimore, Maryland, under one dimly lit hallway lamp, Stewart Sullivan, like a limbering mutt, trudged up the rickety stairs toward his second-floor flat. Each step a reminder that the day had been almost as long as a ten-hour lecture on how to grow corn. Peers would agree; Mr. Sullivan, or Sully, as friends called him, served the bank as an efficient teller, the kind who kept his drawers tight. Like most days, a few impertinent customers, rattling his nerves, led him to the quickest route to peace—the lone bar between work and home, a place where the walls always knew how to speak his language. Now, the temporary peace seemed erased, and he was ninety minutes tardy for supper.

The thirty-four-year-old, thick-bellied man was dressed in a gray suit which clung to him, similar to a bad habit. The rim of his fedora was saturated in sweat. His feet hurt; the bank teller had borne weight on them all day. Suddenly, a smell of over-cooked meatloaf pervaded his nasal cavity, replicating a campfire gone wrong.

"She knows I fucking hate meatloaf...especially scorched," murmured Mr. Sullivan to an audience consisting of only shadows.

Accompanied by a beer buzz, he stood on the worn runner carpet and fiddled at the lock. He shoved the door forward, then lingered over its threshold, statuesque, as if he had somewhere better to be. The unsmiling kitchen table facing him was set for a party of two—engulfed in loneliness.

The barren apartment appeared cluttered and claustrophobic. Mr. Sullivan exhaled a few suffocating breaths, took the fedora off his half-bald, orange-colored hair, and let it sail through the air until it landed with a dull thud on one of the empty plates.

From a bedroom, she emerged, mirroring an aged prizefighter—a little gas remaining in her tank. The woman, decked in a checkered dress and low-heeled pumps, gazed above Sully's round, apricot-shaped nose into his uneasy eyes.

"You're late again, Stew," the comely, auburn-haired wife hissed curtly, "for the third time this week."

"So?"

"Sorry, I burnt dinner," she said.

"Skip the bullshit. Tough day, and you understand I despise meatloaf." His harsh tone blared indignation.

Attempting to mollify his anger, she put her arms around his bulky neck, peered up, fixing her upturned mahogany eyes on him, and chirped, "You didn't always."

"Do now," he replied coldly, gently pushing her back.

He abruptly left the kitchen for the compact den. Once there, he doffed his suit jacket, tossed it onto the floor, loosened his tie, swiveled a knob on a floor-model radio, and then plopped his weight onto the couch.

Mrs. Sullivan tenaciously followed—a bloodhound on a scent. "Are you coming to eat?" she asked, her voice thick with disconsolation.

"Not eating coal," he whined, lying supine. "And besides, the Senators have a night game tonight. Go sew or something."

Seizing the opportune moment, she pivoted her slender frame, found her coat and pocketbook, then made it to the front door, swifter than a three-hundred-pound man could wolf down a spinach pie the size of a fist.

To the slammed door, Mr. Sullivan pleaded briskly, "Sonja, don't leave me again."

For the next three minutes, a stunned Sully laid

there still—a fallen tree in a desolate forest, listening to an announcer talk about Buddy Lewis's batting average. He would soon learn that these three worthless minutes were the biggest mistake of his life.

★   ★   ★

Mr. Sullivan grabbed his hat and barreled down the stairwell, his shoes clattering—echoing fireworks. The door to the street creaked as he pushed it open, exposing him to the inky darkness. Neon signs perched amid the murk, mimicking pink flamingos looking for crustaceans. Deep in the distance, the illumination of the five-hundred-foot former Baltimore Trust Company Building lurked, such as something sinister out of a science fiction movie.

A newsboy, no older than twelve, peddling the evening bulletin and barking out rehearsed headlines, was his first contact. Mr. Sullivan employed a hard stare. "Kid, you spot a dame in a lavender coat?"

The lad tilted his cap, then grinned. "Mista, a lady just hopped inta dat taxi," informed the youth, pointing to a yellow cab a block away, idling at a stoplight.

Mr. Sullivan's jaw tightened, his marital tension gripping him like a vice.

Sully hailed his own hack, one operated by a driver owning a face laced with a patchwork of imperfections. "Tail that taxi. Step on it!" he raspingly growled, striking a palm against the cracked leather of the backseat.

His unsteady fingers lit up a cig, and the ten-minute pursuit began—so did the heavy rain.

Amongst all the zigzags, automobile congestion, and raging downpour, Stewart Sullivan's cab, hauling his glistening misery, lagged behind by a hundred yards. At a corner, he was able to see the evader's yellow door open. Amidst the precipitation, he eyeballed a distorted image of a thin figure running on wet asphalt toward the steps of an unfamiliar apartment complex.

Mr. Sullivan's cigarette smoke filled up the rear of the vehicle, resembling a foggy night. Through the clouds, he leaned forward and asked the cabby, "Why would she come to such a broken neighborhood?" The question he posed may have been better answered by himself, remembering another night when Sonja led him to a place better left forgotten.

"Huh?"

"Never mind. Here's two bucks; keep the change."

Jigsaw Puzzle Face responded, "Thanks, pal! Better go get her."

While running to the corner, Mr. Sullivan caught a flicker of glow from a third-floor residence. By now, his fedora was drenched, clinging to his cranium like a second skin. He peered up and spied the silhouette of a couple dancing—not surreptitiously—in an intimate rhythm on the other side of the drawn window shade. Their bodies seemed intertwined, so close, so tight.

A frown wrinkled his brow as rainwater dribbled down the edges of his mouth, delivering him a bitter taste of one of life's unpleasant fruits.

Why didn't I ever dance with her? he reflected internally, as he intently watched the couple spin aimlessly. The weight of his wet clothes grew heavier following each breath.

★   ★   ★

A middle-aged, beefy, blonde-headed woman wearing a flour-dusted apron waited at the threshold of a German bakery under a canvas awning, hoping for one final customer. The letters "A" and "Y" were unlit in her sign, which simply read "Bakery."

Through the rain, she hollered with urgency, "Zir...Zir, you're goink to catch Pnoo-mohn-ee-ah!"

In the shadows to the right, beneath the same canopy, a short man in a porkpie hat leaned against the brick. His unshaven kisser hid untold secrets; his cigarette burned languidly.

Mr. Sullivan gingerly walked under the awning. To the woman, he sharply questioned, "Who lives up there, third-floor corner pad?" His eyes narrowed, preparing for the unexpected.

"Deh-nee Boy."

"Danny Boy's," Sully forecasted darkly, "gonna get it."

The baker's eyes widened worriedly. She pivoted around and shut the front door of her establishment.

While this was happening, the shorty in the shadows egressed his safe haven, then furtively skulked through the wailing storm, making his way to a phone booth nestled against the building's facade. His teeny body dissolved into the blackness. Mr. Sullivan didn't notice; the magnetism on the third floor kept his frontal lobe preoccupied.

Droplets dripped off the brim of Sully's hat as he nudged the lobby's unlocked door forward and caught soft jazz —bittersweet and haunting—floating to the first-floor lobby.

Meanwhile, the shrimp dropped a nickel into a payphone and, to its mouthpiece, he gravelly divulged, "Looks as if one of Lefty's crew is payin' ya a visit. Might wanna roll out the welcome mat."

Inside the two swaying spirits' apartment, a rough, calloused hand reached out and twisted the volume control of the record player. From below, Sully's elevating ears perceived the abrupt increase in amplitude. It didn't alter his course, each step more burdensome than the last.

If there had been a neighborhood peeper, they would have noticed the lovebirds beyond the shades were no longer lost in their dance. As the anxious husband continued to ascend, water dripped behind him—an omen that he had already gone too far to turn back. Sully's mind, burning like a furnace, spoke: *I'll change, Sonja, I swear it. One more chance.*

When Mr. Sullivan reached the third-floor

landing, the target unit's door appeared slightly ajar, mirroring a fraternity dare. His pulse thumped violently—hands twitching at his sides, poised to strike.

⋆　⋆　⋆

Sully kicked the door open, simulating a police raid, and thrust himself three steps inside the apartment. Fifteen feet ahead, a broad-shouldered bruiser possessing slick black hair leaned lazily against a Crosley stand-up radio, his left elbow propped casually on the device—his right hand hovering near his hip.

As Mr. Sullivan remained motionless with rage carving lines in his phiz, the stranger sarcastically quipped, "Tell Lucky the check's in the mail."

"Lucky? Where's my—?"

Before Sully's mouth could expel the word "wife," the stranger let two hot slugs find a home in the bank teller's gut.

Mr. Sullivan cowered, clutching his abdomen, his visage a mask of pain and shock. "Aargh!" he groaned.

Suddenly, an attractive, redheaded woman sauntered into the living room, movements silent and exact. Her hair shone in the faint light, mimicking a torch in the abyss. She pressed her curves against the bruiser's bulk, who was still standing next to the radio, aiming his revolver at a frozen Sully.

Airing a husky voice, she drawled, "What the hell?"

Mr. Sullivan, guarding his belly, bewilderedly said, "My wife...I thought my wife was here."

To add more chaos to the commotion, the phone booth squirt, out of breath, entered behind Sully and gasped, "Danny Boy, you hurt? Heard shots."

"No, Duke," stated the marksman, Danny Boy, "but we gotta get this guy to an emergency room. He's not connected to Lucky's crew." To Sully, he added, "Don't know your wife from Adam, chum."

The two men, encircled, each placed one of Sullivan's arms over their own shoulders. Bearing most of the weight as his feet dragged, they hauled his limp body downstairs, soldier-like, as if he were a wounded combatant.

Words crawled from Sully's throat as he weakly stammered, "You...you shot me...asshole."

"You trespassed into my house, pal, got the right," countered the lummox called Danny Boy, leading the parade. A trail of blood followed the three men, a winding red river of sorrow.

On the sidewalk, Duke the shrimp hailed a cab.

★   ★   ★

The shooter and his pipsqueak sidekick tossed Sully into the taxi like tomorrow's trash. Sharing a grin capable of cutting glass, the slick-haired bruiser Danny Boy slapped the vehicle's metal roof with one hand and growled, "Take this chump to a hospital, off the meter; no remembering faces, no answering questions," he barked acerbically.

The unfamiliar cabby, owning ghost-white skin

plus big earlobes, twisted his head rearward and incredulously glimpsed at the back seat.

Duke slid the front passenger's door open and floated a twenty down on the seat; the man's eyeballs tracked it.

"Got it," he complied. "Off the meter."

Duke examined the driver's displayed ID, then snarled, "Don't make us come find you."

The wheelman let out an audible gulp, and the short man slammed the door, terminating further conversation.

The unscrupulous duo watched the taxi pull away from the curb into the city's labyrinth of radiance. At the second stoplight, its operator asked, "Mister, you alright?"

"No hospital," Sully uttered softly. "Goin' home, McMechen and Bolton."

"What's happened to you?" The voice was laced in concern.

"Just...some pain," the bank teller murmured. "In my breadbasket.... Drive quick—this'll be...just a bad dream you woke up from...."

Mr. Sullivan shut his eyes.

* * *

For the hack behind the wheel, the ten-minute ride stretched out like a lifetime. "We're here, sir," he announced, voice tight with unease.

Mr. Sullivan's eyes scanned the familiar environment. To the cabby, he advised, "Forget...all...this happened. Stay...out of...it." His words broke apart, ticking sporadically, like a busted watch that could hardly keep time.

Stumbling, Sully barely made it to the entry door before his legs betrayed him. Beyond the threshold, he collapsed as if struck by Knute Rockne's Iron Men of Notre Dame. Exhibiting his last reserve of fortitude, the shooting victim crawled up the stairs, the bullets resting in his gut like a ball and chain dragging him down, each breath a struggle against the weight.

His bleeding followed, a reminder of where his sour disposition had taken him tonight. Using the doorknob like a crutch, he hauled himself to his feet—staggering, unbalanced, akin to an inebriated drunkard.

To his surprise, the door was unlocked. Sully wondered if he'd left it that way.

The spicy odors swirling in the air were pleasant to his nasal cavity. A table set for two seemed welcoming, resembling a perfect dream too fragile to grasp.

In front of the stove, Sonja stood, gracefully stirring something in a skillet, her figure illuminated by the stove's overhead light—an ethereal glow. Above the sizzle, her voice carried vehemently. "I went to Joe's market, and I'm making your favorite: sausage and peppers. Sorry about the meatloaf."

"You're...the only...woman...I've ever...loved... Sonja." As he shallowly muttered, blood spat out of his mouth—an ugly truth which would have saved him an hour ago.

Sully fell to his knees, making a loud thud. Sonja's face twisted in horror as she screamed, "Aaaaiiieee!" Her voice echoed through the halls, bouncing off the walls in an unholy, guttural cry.

She rushed to his side, dropping to her own knees. His gaping wound rapidly dampened her dress. He coughed out a spasm of crimson-colored spew one last time and whispered, "I...think...I'll miss...dinner tonight."

"No! No! Noooooooo!" Sonja shrieked stridently, a desperate prayer that would go unanswered.

9

BLOOD ON HIS HANDS

In Pennsylvania, at 5:10 p.m. on a sultry 1947 September Friday evening, Aram Zakarian, a dandified dresser and fastidious executive at Bethlehem Steel Corporation, briskly operated his '46 Buick Roadmaster, journeying home. The vehicle featured a 320-cubic-inch Fireball Straight-8 engine. It rumbled, akin to a restless beast pleading for speed. And Mr. Zakarian, always the man to indulge a craving, obliged.

The gutsy machine roared down the back road, his private shortcut through the desolate outer grounds of Allentown State Hospital. The pavement was cracked and engulfed by wild shrubbery, a place where the highway patrol turned a deliberate blind eye.

The average-sized, forty-five-year-old Middle Eastern man possessed a khaki-colored face, a thick mustache, and, by this time of day, an inky, five o'clock-shadowed jawline. He sported a wool cranberry suit and a black hat atop a bushel of gray-and-black hair. A gold watch, on his left wrist above the steering wheel, glistened, reminiscent of the opulence of America's defunct Gilded Age.

The Armenian man's egregious driving ritual was to keep his dark eyes on the road for ten seconds, then shift those orbs to a newspaper lying on the seat alongside him.

Meanwhile, two vagrants wearing filthy broadcloth railroad caps shuffled along the shoulder of the empty roadway. Their holey shoes echoed a painful past with each step as they lugged their worldly possessions in over-the-shoulder bindle sacks. Both men were scrawny, gaunt creatures—skeletons wrapped in battered flesh. They trotted in misery, singing off-key, squawking a song as forgotten as yesterday's gossip.

Vagrant #1 ambulated quicker and decided which would be the next tune; it was a tune he could barely remember.

Lagging by ten feet, Vagrant #2's vocal cords cut their harmony. "Gots to pee," he muttered, scanning the horizon warily for his desired spot.

Vagrant #2 found the bushes. Vagrant #1 kept marching until the speeding automobile's bumper clobbered him in the ass. His ragdoll frame stuck to it, blocking Mr. Zakarian's view. The machine skidded erratically off the cement with Mr. Zakarian employing the brakes, but only slowing it down. It struck a telephone pole, leaving the hobo caught in between, like sandwich meat. A life-ending paroxysm of extremity jerks came simultaneously with a tidal wave of useless blood moving northward to his upper body.

A horrified Mr. Zakarian's gaze became fixed on the backside of the man glued to the pole, whose posterior head ballooned outward, mirroring an inflatable beach ball. Not the kind you'd want to kick.

Mr. Zakarian tensely eased the car into reverse, rolling back a good five yards, then got out. The perpetrator's kisser quivered as his bushy eyebrows jolted skyward, viewing a motionless man lying supine below him, one who exhibited a crushed pelvis and ribs.

Next, Zakarian twisted his head in all directions but saw no one. He looked low again, this time at his vehicle's front passenger-side whitewall tire, currently stained crimson.

This'll land me behind bars...involuntary manslaughter. They'll know I wasn't even close to the road, he reflected internally. A chill crawled up his spine.

The dead vagrant's bindle sack hung on the Buick's hood ornament—a lantern of mortality. The office executive removed it and callously dropped it over the corpse. Subsequently, Mr. Zakarian pulled on the now crooked bumper; it was buckled but secure. The grill on top appeared as if its teeth had been kicked in.

Finishing his business, Vagrant #2 heard the *wham*. It yanked his puny body out into the open. Viewing his flattened chum caused a grim expression to show upon his unshaven countenance—one already laced with anguish.

"Hey," Mr. Zakarian hollered angrily to the frozen, waiflike man, forty feet up the embankment, "it was an accident!"

Vagrant #2 morosely stared for five seconds at the chaos he'd stumbled across, then ran, mimicking an army deserter amidst the shrubbery, and kept going yonder.

Mr. Zakarian felt his nerves fraying like cheap thread. He had three choices: chase the man, report the incident, or navigate away from the macabre scene he created. He chose the latter—an unmistakable dereliction of duty.

Before fleeing he made sure that he caked mud on the lone license plate affixed to the rear bumper, making its three numbers and two letters illegible.

★   ★   ★

Mr. Zakarian's sled coughed and sputtered as it limped into the driveway, his own hands trembling as he attempted to shake off the weight of his conscience. The Roadmaster's hood coughed enough steam to resemble a dragon from a seven-year-old's favorite fairy tale and enough to catch the attention of his next-door neighbor, Elmer Kowalski, sitting on the sagging porch of the only dilapidated home in the district.

The apex of the onlooker's head was shiny and bald, with the unruly surviving blonde hair clinging to the sides, desperately trying to hold on. Kowalski wore ungodly tight, cream-colored pants, plus an undershirt over his pot belly, mirroring a towel covering a bowling ball.

Mr. Zakarian, rising to his feet, nodded as a nonverbal greeting. The man returned no greeting at all.

Suddenly, the front door of Zakarian's brick house flung open. A fit woman came outside who would've passed for the queen of Persia. She showcased black, silky hair, and bold, thick eyebrows that enhanced her amber-toned eyes, allowing them to shimmer like warm desert sand. The kind of eyes which could mesmerize a man into obedience, or stupefy his thoughts. She wore a yellow, sleeveless cotton dress, decorated at its base by a multicolored floral brocade, plus beige, high-heeled mules, making her painted toes look prominent.

"What the hell's going on with the car?" she asked, flummoxed, gazing at the clouds of smoke. "It's still new." The exquisite lady's throaty voice, given to her by her maker, carried a doting undertone, as though laced with concern.

"Radiator's overheating."

"Aram, the bumper is dented."

"Let's chat in private," he cautioned.

To their bald, gawking neighbor, Zabel Zakarian glowered and chided, "And what the hell are you peepin' at?"

As the couple strolled up the cobblestone walkway, the Armenian housewife threw her arms in the air and revealed, "That creep was staring at me over the fence while I was putting clothes on the line today."

"Zabel, I'll talk to his mother."

"Aram, what kind of forty-year-old man lives in his mother's basement?"

"I said I'd talk to his mother. Listen, we have bigger problems," he replied, attempting to avert Zabel from further argument. "Come inside."

★   ★   ★

On Saturday morning, wearing a pink robe, Zabel Zakarian brought in the newspaper, *The Morning Call.* Its top headline: *"Local Police Searching for Deadly Hit-and-Run Driver: No Leads Yet."*

She plopped the folded paper in front of her husband's scrambled eggs. "Go see my brother," she advised.

★   ★   ★

In Allentown's 6th Ward, down by the Lehigh River in a gritty section tagged as Little Syria, sat a bush-league operation called Kevork's Auto Body and Sales.

Mr. Zakarian eased the big Buick through the gap

in the sagging chain-link fence. Its radiator fumed, exhausting all the water that was added prior to the trip. The steel executive stepped out, straightened his suit jacket, and pushed open the door of the shabby office, its paint peeling, bearing resemblance to the last remnants of his own dignity.

The joint smelled like stale cigarettes. Sitting behind a dented metal desk was a bulky, oval-headed, partially balding man with a chiseled chin, sporting a gold chain as thick as a baby rattlesnake. Mr. Zakarian's eyes studied his brother-in-law, Kevork, basking in all his glory—a jack-of-all-trades thug, a good soul to have in your corner.

"Sell ya a jalopy?" ribbed Kevork, offering a handshake—one that could break your phalanges if the recipient wasn't careful.

"No time for jokes. I possess troubles," Aram Zakarian made known, blatantly staring at a grease stain on the hulk's white shirt.

"Zabel phoned. Secret's safe wit' me."

"I need a new radiator, grill, and bumper, pronto."

"Give me until next week."

"Monday."

"Eh?"

"Cops are going to be prowling around," Zakarian warned, pointing outside, "and there was a witness."

"That's bad."

Mr. Zakarian fished inside his wallet, then set down a stack of bills in front of the mechanic.

Reversing his syntax, Kevork uttered, "That's good."

"Monday," reiterated Zakarian.

"Yeah, but can't find one in a junkyard. It's a '46, right?"

Within seconds, Aram Zakarian increased the altitude of the stack of greenbacks. "Have one of your contacts steal one if necessary; take off the goods, keep some for yourself, then scrap or burn it."

"You're askin' a lot." After he said it, the shady businessman gawked at the bills and cast an enigmatic smile.

"I know of your scoundrelly associates, Kevork, and I also understand you've been cheating on your wife, Anoush."

"Whoa!" The bigger man thudded a fist on his desk. "That's bull."

"A frail," Zakarian rasped, standing erect, "down in Hazleton."

Kevork's expression turned deadpan.

Mr. Zakarian resumed, "Got a child by her, I hear."

Kevork paused for a second, then negotiated. "We both carry secrets."

"Help me with mine, Kevork."

"Who's the witness?"

"Some vagrant, probably on an outbound freight car by now."

Kevork nodded in agreement. "Pick up the chariot Monday mornin'. Let's get you a lift home."

*   *   *

Monday afternoon driving home, the repaired Buick felt almost as good as new to Aram Zakarian, who took a circuitous route around the state hospital grounds, avoiding the crime scene.

At a deceptively calm intersection where he would normally exit the sanatorium's back road, Vagrant #2 stood on the sidewalk, looking like a scarecrow—eyes squinting, features hollow, rags blowing faintly in the breeze. Unsure if he'd been seen, Zakarian fretfully gazed straight ahead. His foot hovered over the gas pedal for a split second, then he slammed it down, sending the Buick lurching forward toward home.

*   *   *

A day later, at an intersection closer to his residence, Zakarian noticed Vagrant #2—a lone wolf—loitering in the periphery, his eyes darting from car to car as he patiently searched for one in particular.

*   *   *

Wednesday, the rain fell steadily, and the Roadmaster's squeaking wipers danced in rhythm. At an intersection even closer to home, Mr. Zakarian caught sight of something too familiar for comfort. The stranger's uncanny third consecutive appearance caused his bones to rattle It wasn't merely coincidence anymore; it was a warning. His grip tightened on the steering wheel, knuckles white, as a shiver crawled down his spine.

He's trying to pinpoint where I hang my hat, he mused, the words tasting worse than ash in his mouth. He swung the ride to the curb and killed its ignition. He got out, then approached a soaking wet Vagrant #2 sitting on a boulder the size of a chuck wagon.

"How much?"

"Fuh what?" replied the stranger, airing a harsh voice like a rusty blade from a lifetime of inhaling cigarettes.

"To leave town."

"Uh-huh. You're gonna git yours. It's a baby."

Mr. Zakarian perceived the stranger's words to be tangential. Before he could utter a word in return, a patrol car pulled up.

The gray-haired portly officer, too long on the job, rolled down his window. To Mr. Zakarian, he asked, "Is there a problem here, sir?"

To the uniform, Mr. Zakarian said, "Just seeing if this feller required any help." The executive's vertebrae stiffened, a flicker of annoyance flashing in his eyes

To Vagrant #2, the officer gruffly bellowed, "Find the train tracks! Beat it!" His tone was acerbic—intolerant.

Once the relic in the prowl car was out of earshot,

Mr. Zakarian leaned into his stalker's face and whispered three words he had never uttered together: "I'll kill you." Rain dripped off the brim of his fedora like it was spilling from a roof's corroded gutter as he walked back to the Buick.

* * *

Thursday, 5:30 p.m., Mr. Zakarian, dressed in a crisp blue suit he'd paid plenty for, drove home from his office at Bethlehem Steel, his heart rattling in his chest, mimicking a loose piston.

"Where's this creep going to be today?" he edgily muttered to the steering wheel.

As his turnoff came into view, a flicker of relief washed over him.

The feeling was short-lived, akin to a birthday candle. Under a yellow stop sign at the corner of his street stood a rail-thin, ghostly man supporting a bindle over a bony shoulder. Zakarian's initial thoughts were to keep accelerating and leave the phantom in his rearview mirror, but a voice in his head growled, *He's too close to my bunk. This ends now.*

At the seventh house, Mr. Zakarian zoomed the automobile into his driveway, leaving its door ajar like a wobbly tooth. He briefly saw his bald-headed neighbor, Elmer Kowalski, mirroring a buzzard, perched on his own rickety porch.

Conspicuously, Vagrant #2 trailed on foot, stopping at the second dwelling, beholding all he needed to.

At the front door, donned in an orange rayon dress with white leaves, Zabel Zakarian cordially greeted her husband. "I cooked a big dish of dolma for you, Aram."

Mr. Zakarian ignored his pretty wife, barging past her. He reached inside a bureau drawer, abruptly pulling out a gleaming .38 pistol.

She followed. "Aram, what the hell are you doing?" Zabel barked, her voice loud enough to chisel into his rage. "Where did you acquire the gun?"

"Kevork, your wonderful brother." Next, Aram Zakarian answered her first question by explaining his contorted plan, steeped in malice. "That second vagrant is at the corner, stalking me." He slapped the nearest wall and maliciously resumed, "I'm going to shoot him, throw the carcass in my trunk, then dump it in our living room when it grows dark in an hour. I'll tell the cops he broke in. It's an easy way to get away with murder, then this all disappears."

Zabel tugged at his sleeve, her hand trembling, eyes wide with fear, mouth slightly agape as she tried to process his words. "Please, Aram, no. Do you hear what you are saying? This is madness!" she cried. "Don't you see? This whole thing has made you evil! Go to the cops, tell 'em the truth!"

"Outta my path!" shouted the executive-gone-maniac, brushing by her shoulder.

The engine hummed a low, ominous tune as Mr. Zakarian drove the six hundred or so feet to the corner. *I'll offer him a ride*, he sinisterly thought, casting a crooked grin, *and bombard him with lead.*

When he reached it, Vagrant #2 had been swallowed by the evening shadows—nowhere to be found.

★   ★   ★

Forty-five minutes later, after cruising around town in circles in a pointless waltz, Mr. Zakarian returned home. Dusk had begun to set on the Allentown community. The temperature now aired at a brisk fifty degrees. His mood had cooled off as well, regret gnawing at his inner self. *Going to tell Zabel I was out of my head.*

He unlocked the front door and stepped inside. The usual hum of Zabel's genial welcome seemed strangely absent. *She's probably out looking for me*, he thought indifferently. Zakarian casually tossed his suit jacket on the sofa, but the coolness in the living room made him think he needed it back. *She must have left a window open. That's it.*

He entered the kitchen, and the chilly draft greeted him, bearing the grim cadence of a cemetery march. A knot twisted in his gut—the window was open alright, but pried open in a way only a carpenter could fix.

The utter violation provoked him to pull out the .38 revolver and run down the hallway, stepping over a pack of cigarettes—Zabel's cigarettes. The bedroom door was ajar. He flicked the light on, and there she lay on the bed, unrecognizable, in a supine position.

He hopped onto the bed, kneeling beside what was left of her, and gently released the firearm. He slid one arm under her neck, the other under her knees, then curled her torso upwards like a weight-lifter. Her skin still felt warm, but her sliced-up body was lifeless.

Covered in her blood, to an audience of none, he screamed, "Zabel, how could I leave our castle unprotected! Your blood is on my hands!"

Those sanguineous hands dripped as he staggered to the kitchen, picked up the receiver, and called the police department.

*   *   *

Friday morning at 10 a.m., beyond the façade of archaic bricks, a disheveled man shuffled into the police station. His putrid armpit odor would have paralyzed even the most experienced dumpster diver.

Vagrant #2 stood in front of an unoccupied counter. A tall blonde cop, displaying badge number twenty-two, walked by, pinching his nose, and snickered, "Smitty's takin' a piss. You can confess your sins to him when he's finished." The officer then burst through the exit doors, jumped into a cruiser, and vamoosed.

Vagrant #2 hovering at the desk sergeant's vacant post and chanted, "Dum, dum, dum," a song he invented all by himself. Soon, he plopped a folded piece of paper on the counter and made himself gone, like Clara Bow's movie career.

*   *   *

At noon, in the same precinct, a broad-shouldered detective who went by O'Reilly cast a steel-gray glare across his desk. He was an irascible lion of a man, possessing big fists, the kind that looked as if they had landed on a few nasal bones. O'Reilly sported a flat-top haircut featuring shaved sides, a blue tie, and a white dress shirt with the sleeves rolled up to his jagged elbows

Blotched, broken capillaries from whiskey dependence lined his phiz like a Phillips 66 road map to nowhere. Atop a granite jaw, a cynical smile existed, a half-smoked cigarette dangling out of it.

On the other side of the desk, breathing in a plethora of secondhand smoke, Aram Zakarian, a shipwreck, sat with his hands buried in his face, sobbing through bloodshot eyes. He wore yesterday's dress shirt as wrinkled as a geisha girl's bamboo fan.

"You must know something," growled Detective O'Reilly, his voice sandpaper rough, his words always transparent.

Mr. Zakarian stared at the gun in the policeman's shoulder holster, a cold, silent reminder of the brute who could make his life even worse.

"Came home from work," Zakarian sniffled, pitching his voice barely above a whisper, "and found her butchered."

O'Reilly's eyes exhibited sympathy as he paused for five seconds.

"Want one?" asked the detective, pointing at a pack of Camel cigarettes.

"Don't smoke," responded Zakarian flatly.

"Were there any affairs?" O'Reilly asked, wielding a gaze sharp as a scalpel, cutting the air in the room between the two men. "You need to tell me now."

"Not that I'm aware of," murmured the recent widower, drying his weeping eyes, utilizing a handkerchief.

"Hmmm."

"Do you think it may have been an intruder, robbing our roost, and found my wife home alone?"

"No," O'Reilly theorized. "This is personal; she was stabbed fifty times."

It's personal, alright, Zakarian thought. *It's because of me.*

Detective O'Reilly figured it was time to gingerly interrogate suspect number one. "Your whereabouts," he imparted curtly, "are a little sketchy. They said you left work a little after five, but you didn't phone in the murder until six thirty."

"I drove down to the Lehigh Valley Parkway. I sit near the bridge sometimes. Forgot to eat lunch Friday, so I brought it there."

"At five thirty? That sounds like marriage trouble to me." O'Reilly gauchely spat out his cigarette butt in an ashtray. "And didn't your wife have supper waiting for you? They found it uneaten during the search."

"I simply wanted to relax on a bench following work."

Zakarian was slumping deeper into his chair—a man trying to slip through the cracks of the earth itself, leading him to a darker place. The detective keenly noticed every inch of the liar's slow descent. It empowered him.

"Well, there's another matter," O'Reilly stated, "that led us to bring you in today."

"Huh?"

Detective O'Reilly laconically dropped an opened piece of paper with several creases in front of his potential suspect. He watched as Mr. Zakarian, hands shaking like a leaf in a storm, picked it up and nervously read the sloppy note, containing multiple spelling errors.

The killa of Sami on the hosputel grounz lives in the 7 hous on Jazman Lain. the brik one.

It was unsigned.

"Seems as though a six-year-old kid wrote this scribble. Wonder why? Do you know any six-year-olds?"

"No, sir."

The detective lit up an additional cig, then blew the initial cloud toward the ceiling. "Funny, you live in a brick house on Jasmin Lane, the seventh one. And a vagrant carrying an ID with the name Samuel was a hit-and-run victim a week ago today. Care to explain that?"

I should've ditched the hobo's bag, Zakarian pondered, then said, "But, detective, the note reads 'Jazman.'"

"You're a comedian. I told you it was written by a six-year-old."

"I'm just a grieving husband, sir."

Another five minutes of routine inquires followed, which were as helpful to the detective as a field goal when your team is trailing by forty points. The brawny lawman finally rose to a standing position.

"Can't hold you," he conveyed, "but we gotta check out your ride. Leave it here. Don't skip town. We have two unsolved murders in this city, and somehow your name is connected to both."

From the lobby of the grimy precinct, Mr. Zakarian caught sight of a brown-haired rookie flaunting badge number fifty-five, still green out of the academy, pushing a man up the front steps in cuffs. Zakarian lingered, his gaze flickering over the most wanted posters, imagining his own face among them.

The prisoner had his head bowed.

"Toss him in the cooler," directed Smitty, a burly desk sergeant who presented as a man who took too many lunch breaks. "He can see the judge on Monday."

The valves in Mr. Zakarian's cardiac muscle were fluttering, analogous to a butterfly's wings. He recognized that dirty cap. The prisoner was Vagrant #2.

★   ★   ★

Aram Zakarian, sinking in misery, made a phone call, and fifteen minutes later, two beefy arms operating the steering wheel of a '45 Ford truck picked him up in front of the police station. The engine's grumble matched the squall brewing in Aram's gut.

Kevork, the brother of Aram's murdered wife, was the driver. His Middle Eastern visage appeared filled with rage. His fists pounded the dashboard like anvils, displaying an impetuous temperament. He sported a V-neck undershirt, and the visible chest hair looked so dense that a clan of mice could have hidden in it.

"Get in!" he ordered. "Tell me my sistuh Zabel's death doesn't connect to your little problem last week." His dark eyes burned holes into the widower.

"That witness did it—the second vagrant," Zakarian gravely divulged, descending to the passenger's seat. "He cleverly found my house, killed her, then left a jotted message at the police station, snitching on me for running down his friend."

"How can this become any worse?" yelled Kevork frantically, still applying his foot on the brake. "How can I find this piece of shit?"

"He's locked up in a holding tank under the police station."

"How do you know that?"

"They're detaining him 'til court Monday morning on a vagrancy charge."

"I got," blurted Kevork, "an idea. You're gonna do exactly as I tell ya to. Must pick up somethin' at the auto body shop on the way."

★   ★   ★

Saturday, 4 p.m., standing out front of a joint called the Last Resort Pool Hall, Kevork Harootunian rehearsed his sinister scenario alongside his dupe, Aram Zakarian.

"Let's go ovuh this one more time," said Kevork. "You're gonna strike my man Timmy ovuh the noggin' usin' a cue stick, nice and easy. Then the bartender, Chip, is gonna call the fuzz. Meanwhile, ya sit at the bar and act rowdy."

Mr. Zakarian attentively bobbed his head in compliance.

Kevork resumed, "Before the cops get there, I'm gonna give ya a rubbuh glove filled wit' powduh. Ya stick it deep in your unduhpants. I know at this station they hardly frisk ya and only remove your suit pants. They'll return the pants once they checked the pockets. Keep the glove tucked unduh your nuts."

Mr. Zakarian grew wide-eyed as he listened further.

"This precinct," Kevork added, "has a few bunks and one big holdin' cell, so our hobo friend will be sittin' pretty. Grab him by the back of the neck and cake his nose in powduh. He takes a few good breaths, then it's goodbye."

"What if your poisonous compound doesn't work?"

"It will," replied Kevork. "And it will look like he died of a heart attack. Make sure ya clean the powduh off his face. Soon enough, they'll release ya because Timmy from the bar will drop the battery charge."

* * *

The Last Resort Pool Hall was a low-rent dive that stank of stale beer and cheap sausage, the kind of place you visit after dreams die. Eight days ago, it wouldn't have been Zakarian's cup of tea.

Seeing his situation spiraling out of control, the lost soul did as he was told: struck some cat named Timmy's cranium lightly and acted like a jerk.

When the two uniformed flatfoots finally showed up, Zakarian kept doggedly banging an open palm on the bar, pretending to be inebriated.

He slurred, "Arrest me, who gives a shit!"

One of the cops—a boyish-faced rookie Zakarian recognized from the earlier haul-in of Vagrant #2—barreled his way toward the bar.

To the bartender, Chip, carrying the frowsy kisser of a thousand hangovers, the young officer remarked, "I take it this is the guy."

"Yup," confirmed Ole Red Face, giving a lazy nod and pouring a beer for a sulking patron sporting a cowboy hat.

The cuffs clicked, and Mr. Zakarian was marched out like someone straight off one of those wanted posters he had examined a few hours prior.

⋆   ⋆   ⋆

Employing an impatient and firm grip, the wet-behind-the-ears cop muscled a shackled Aram Zakarian into the grungy station in the same fashion as he had Vagrant #2 hours ago.

They trudged down the stairs toward the dim basement, which reeked of mildew, a stench worse than a burly athlete's discarded jockstrap.

Approaching a holding cell fit for maybe ten prisoners, the bluecoat sarcastically warned, "Watch yourself, he hears voices."

Mr. Zakarian was shoved into the cage violently. In a far corner, cocooned up in a ball, lay the only other prisoner, Vagrant #2, self-dialoguing some gibberish no sane man would try to unravel.

The rookie locked the gate with a clang, nodded once, and disappeared up the stairs.

Zakarian wasted no time. He pivoted around, his eyes cold as slate, and planted a swift kick in the vagrant's back. The startled man's puny frame jumped to a sitting position. The drifter peered way up at the man who treated his only friend like garbage.

"I know," said Vagrant #2, "where you live."

"Obviously!" hollered Zakarian, as he reached into his underpants and yanked out the rubber glove—a bloated, knotted pouch containing the toxic powder. Zakarian broke the glove's knot and placed it, ripped open, on the long wooden bench. An effluvium pervaded the air.

Advancing to a kneeling position and casting a countenance of horror, Vagrant #2 stammered, "What...What's that?"

"Your last meal," snarled Zakarian, grabbing the posterior portion of the gaunt man's neck, pushing his snout into the pile of lethal poison.

The victim, flailing weak upper extremities attempting to claw at his attacker, spluttered and wheezed. Zakarian then scooped up a fistful of granules and, using two fingers, brutally jammed them deep inside Vagrant #2's nares. The man fell rearward, unconscious, his skull viciously meeting the unforgiving concrete floor.

Next, Zakarian slumped to his knees, then started wiping the noxious substance off the vagrant's nose as instructed—a delicate chore. Within seconds, the supposed corpse expelled a mammoth sneeze, and powder sailed at Zakarian, mimicking ghostly vapor. It gave the palate inside his oral cavity the sourest taste he had ever experienced. Zakarian himself, forcefully hacking up sputum, involuntarily flopped beside the man.

A minute passed, and when Zakarian came to, he perceived more coughing—Vagrant #2's coughing.

The powder didn't work, Mr. Zakarian fretfully pondered.

Mr. Zakarian fiercely rose to a standing position and, with fury, dragged Vagrant #2's weakened body toward the wall. Next, his two vengeful hands gripping the gasping man's nape, Zakarian savagely pounded his enemy's frontal lobe against the corner of the wooden bench.

"Die...die!" yelled the madman. He kept pounding until he no longer heard gasping, and the vagrant's skull caved like a rotten fruit.

Mr. Zakarian pushed his victim's lifeless shell beneath the bench, arranging him as if the poor sap had drifted off for a nap. The executioner then sat on the cold floor with his back slumped, resting upon the hard wood that had just killed a man. He cried like some folks do after a movie's sad ending.

Once the well ran dry, and his eyes were just as empty as his conscience, Zakarian muttered to himself, *Have to skip town as soon as they unlock that door.*

⋆   ⋆   ⋆

In the bowels of the ancient precinct, Detective O'Reilly, carrying a frame dense as a brick warehouse, marched down the dim corridor, unlocked the iron door, then strode into the cage.

His steel-gray eyes found Mr. Zakarian. "Got two

pieces of news," he informed, airing a grizzly voice and grasping a fist around an iron bar. "Your neighbor, Elmer Kowalski, whom we've been interrogating, came clean and confessed to violating and then murdering your wife."

Disregarding his own sin, the widower glimpsed up and exclaimed, "Kowalski, that bastard!"

"He's a known Peeping Tom to us." O'Reilly paused, his hard eyes softening merely a fraction. "My condolences, Mr. Zakarian."

The detainee perched at the edge of the bench, ten feet from the curled-up dead man, bobbed his head up and down. "Thank you, Detective," he replied, cloaking a tone as somber as a midnight alley. Mr. Zakarian wanted to throw a tantrum, but his mind spoke instead. *If I hadn't gone chasing this bum, Zabel would he still be alive. He deserved what he got.*

The detective situated himself halfway into the cage. His face hardened, similar to an asphalt jungle. He resumed, "Gonna let you out now. The guy you roughed up at the billiard parlor ain't pressing charges." O'Reilly pointed a beefy finger, showing authority. "Don'tcha leave the area. We still have the issue with that six-year-old's note. Our criminalistics investigator is gonna tear through your car tomorrow morning."

"*Bye, bye. I'll be on the next train outta this shit hole,*" whispered Zakarian under his breath as he hopped to his feet, muscles aching from the scuffle. To the detective, he mumbled, "I understand."

O'Reilly supinated his hand. "You're free to go, Mr. Zakarian."

The words were euphonious to the killer's ears. He started walking out of the lockup. As he did, O'Reilly looked at Vagrant #2's body, coiled below the bench, and joked, "Your cellie here is another Rip Van Winkle."

"Yeah, not much company," uttered Zakarian, hastily heading to the exit stairs.

The tall blonde cop wearing badge number twenty-two, who had brushed by Vagrant #2 earlier, descended the stairs. His steps, heavy with purpose, met an ascending Zakarian halfway along the stairwell. "Hold on," directed the uniformed copper as—unbeknownst to him—he plowed a murderer backward.

O'Reilly joined the duo, and the three men loomed, resembling marble statues at the foot of the stairs.

To Detective O'Reilly, the tall, blonde officer stated, "Just got off my detail. I told Smitty upstairs a vagrant delivered that chicken-scratch note with this guy's address on it." He jabbed a finger, sharp as an arrow, toward Zakarian when he said it. The golden-headed lawman resumed, "I saw the vagabond on my way out, around ten this morning, lingering around Sergeant Smitty's lair."

"And?" hissed O'Reilly.

"Smitty sent me down here to make sure the pieces click."

Mr. Zakarian began to perspire like a lava pit.

"So, it wasn't a kid who wrote it?" O'Reilly skeptically questioned his associate.

"No."

"Zimmerman," Detective O'Reilly inquired, pointing downward inside the cell, "was it this vagrant?"

The lofty German patrolman's eyes followed. "Yeah, that's him," responded the tall, blonde officer.

"The bum was arrested," O'Reilly imparted, "downtown, waving at traffic around noon."

Mr. Zakarian had heard enough. Applying a sudden, desperate twist, he tried to wrest himself free from Officer Zimmerman's brass clutch. But Zimmerman, a grizzled veteran serving fifteen hard years on the force, wasn't about to let him escape. The enforcer maneuvered Zakarian into the cell and pinned him to the far-right side of the wooden bench.

Immediately succeeding the skirmish, Detective O'Reilly entered the lawless pen. To Zakarian and his captor, he said, "Gonna dig to the bottom of this right now." He sniffed his nostrils twice. "And what's that faint chemical smell in here?"

The question went unanswered as Zakarian squirmed under Zimmerman's hold.

O'Reilly dropped to one knee and slid a hand

under the left portion of the bench. "Rise and shine, pal!" he growled, his voice akin to a bullhorn.

The dead man lay on his side, tucked with his back to the entrance. At first, O'Reilly applied a little nudge, then began shaking the cadaver vigorously by his dirty shirt. "Hey. Hey, what happened here?"

The lightbulb above flickered as the detective energetically dragged the expired flesh into the middle of the unforgiving tomb.

Zakarian, still being held against his will, screamed, "I didn't do anything! Let me go!"

The rugged detective placed Vagrant #2's body supine and methodically examined the man, recently reduced to a shell. "What did you do to his head? He's not breathing...he's...gone!" The sclera of O'Reilly's sockets were red with fury. Turning to Zakarian, he roared vehemently, "Buddy, you'll get the chair. The blood of two transient men is on your hands!"

10

SILENT MOVIE STAR

September '47, Los Angeles, California. The room acridly stank of cigarette smoke and cheap whiskey. Peeling wallpaper, a once-proud shade of amber, hung in strips, adding to the dreariness of the place. The only illumination came from a broken lamp, casting lengthy, lurid shadows across the cramped, rundown apartment. It wasn't much, but it was his, and that's about all Silas Mercer could say for his life these days.

Mr. Mercer was fifty-one, worn at the edges. His elongated, non-mustached kisser sagged at the jowls, cheeks pitted, bearing resemblance to an old sidewalk. Oily skin caught the light at all the wrong angles. Brown eyes sat deep and solemn below a furrowed brow, and gray had already won the color battle in his hair. Ears stuck out just enough to be memorable.

A potbelly strained his belt, and a pointy chin jutted forward, stubborn as an errant screw.

He sat hunched over, his sagging shoulders like a slump of wet cement, beadily glancing at the newspaper spread out on the table. The headline appeared exiguous, the photo grainy—no glitz, no glamour, merely a faded image of a woman past her prime. It didn't matter. He knew her face as well as he knew his own.

Lila Varnay—The Velvet Starlet Resurfaces
in Ogden, Utah.

"So, that's where the bitch is hiding," Silas mumbled gruffly under his breath. His fingers tightened around the paper, crumpling its margins before tossing it aside carelessly.

Beside Silas, a pudgy woman ten years his junior lazily slouched in a threadbare armchair, nursing a glass half-filled with bourbon. Makeup was smudged, golden hair limp. Dull orbits carried the sheen of too many nights spent drinking troubles away. Gaudy perfume—the kind that assaulted your nostrils—enveloped her. She wore a gossamer robe, a bra and panties veiled beneath. Ruby...yeah, that was her name. He couldn't recall if he'd ever really fancied her. She was okay for a few perks—mainly, keeping her mouth shut when it mattered.

The floozy tilted her noggin back, squinting

toward the paper, her false lashes hanging on for dear life. "Lila Varnay," she muttered. "*Velvet Shadows.* I remember that flick—before the talkies, huh?"

Silas Mercer's lips curled into a grimace. "Yeah. *Velvet Shadows.* It's what did me in."

Ruby offered a sloppy nod, swigging from the bottle. Her voice aired hoarse, like a frog who'd been smoking raw cigarettes for twenty years. "What...what happened?"

Mercer's jaw tightened. "That bitch said I cornered her in her dressing room. 'Trespassed,' she called it. It wasn't true, though. I was simply trying to make conversation. The broad kept eyeing me between takes, playing a game, you follow? I gave the camera a break and—"

"And you knocked," Ruby interrupted, dragging a shaky hand through her tangled hair, wearily, eyes rolling faintly.

"Yeah. I knocked. That's it," Silas hissed, his face growing redder by the second. "She made a fuss. Claimed I was a stalker. Next thing I know, I'm out on my ass. Hollywood's up-and-coming lensman, booted outta Tinsel Town 'cause she couldn't keep her goggling orbs to herself."

Ruby laughed; a dry, wheezing rasp, which sent fury down Silas's spine. "What happened to her?" asked the trollop.

"Varnay's career fizzled when the talkies came in," he growled, his breath thick with venom. "They found out her vocal cords sounded like a damn hyena on a hot day. She vanished after the late twenties. Haven't heard a peep since."

Ruby rubbed at her blotched temples, words slurring as she reached for the bottle again. "I need another drink."

"Yeah, yeah," Silas grumbled, getting up from the chair, knees cracking. He threw on his windbreaker, which had seen better days, and headed out the door.

The street seemed dim, the neon bulbs scarcely cutting through the smog. It was a short stroll to the corner liquor store, but the walk wasn't what bothered him. It was a nagging thought in his skull, the one lingering there ever since he'd viewed that blasted article.

When he returned, Ruby tarried in the same spot, barely moving, her glass empty. She gazed up at him, blinking drowsily.

"You look upset," she remarked, garbling her words.

Silas didn't answer initially. He just stood in position, his vertebrae stiff, staring down at her unemotionally. A slow, cruel smile unfurled across his face as he plopped the bottle on the tabouret.

"Yeah, Ruby, I've been thinking. Thinking it's a damn good time for me to take a trip to Ogden, Utah."

Mr. Mercer reckoned the trip would have to be a solo one.

★ ★ ★

Sunlight bathed Ogden, the sky clear and untouched. Utah's mountains, stoic guardians, towered prominently around the town, their jagged peaks rending the horizon as if to shield the busy streets below. A 1933 Rolls-Royce wheezed painfully alongside a curb, the last remnant of her Hollywood mansion, foreclosed the same year—five years after her final movie. She kept the automobile because she could never afford another. Built for American roads, the left-hand drive vehicle coughed exhaust, echoing that of an old drunkard.

Lila Varnay sat languidly in the back, a svelte woman draped in a silk scarf and oversized hat, sunglasses so dark they eclipsed her face. Fine lines etched the years upon her mouth, but her chin remained high, as it had when cameras once adored her.

"Well, Henshaw," she snapped sharply, barely turning her head toward the driver, "are you waiting for the mayor to roll out a carpet? Go on!"

The chauffeur, Walter Henshaw—white-haired and hunch-spined—climbed out, not uttering a word. He'd long stopped trying to argue. Varnay sent him in everywhere—grocers, pharmacies, laundry, and dry goods. A woman such as Lila Varnay didn't loiter aimlessly in dime stores, not even in a place like Ogden.

She resolutely stayed put, knuckles restless against

the upholstery, scanning the street from beyond her lenses. If anyone recognized her, they didn't say so. Maybe they were too young. Maybe they simply disdained her smugness.

By the time Mr. Henshaw reappeared with a small bag, her scowl had already hardened.

"You certainly dragged your feet," Varnay said sarcastically, a barb edged with impatience. She plucked a cigarette from a gold case and stuck it in a Bakelite holder. "Did you forget how to walk?"

The old man didn't respond, just shimmied behind the wheel. She fancied that about him. Silence. It gave space to think, to reminisce about what it was like when folks rushed to her, fawned over her. Now, realizing the world had moved on without her, she unleashed today's frustrations on a tired chap who only needed a job.

Lila Varnay exhaled a leisurely stream of smoke and settled comfortably in the seat. "Drive," she murmured dully, waving a palm dismissively, flicking ash into a glass.

The car rolled forward, and Lila Varnay disappeared deeper into a town that had other things to do than harbor a washed-up star.

★ ★ ★

Silas Mercer entered the cluttered pawn shop, his conscience lighter than his pockets. He reckoned Ruby would serve some purpose eventually. He laid her prized possessions dispassionately on the counter—a gold necklace and two rings—watching the scrawny, silver-haired clerk assess their value with the scrutiny of a butcher inspecting spoiled meat.

Fifty bucks. Silas silenced his trap, snatched the bills, tucked them inside a battered wallet, and faded into the city's glare.

Union Station was populated—uniformed soldiers returning from leave carrying duffel bags, businessmen, housewives clutching their purses, and unscrupulous individuals owning eyes analogous to his, searching for an easy way out. Silas preferred a crowd. It made him anonymous. He found a seat on the Los Angeles Limited, stretching out in the manner of a man hauling revenge in lieu of a suitcase, and he stored it on his mind unwaveringly all the way to Utah.

* * *

Her name was Mildred—thin as a dime and definitely as common. She resentfully got ready for her Monday job, the one that festered in her belly like a bad meal. It wasn't the work; she'd done worse. It was Lila Varnay, the woman who hired her—one endowed with a taste for pitilessly making those in her presence squirm.

A couple of months ago, Mildred owned a car. Then some fling named Ronald drove off with it, including whatever promises he'd falsely created.

Since then, every Monday afternoon, she begrudgingly burned shoe leather, plodding the one-mile trek to Varnay's estate.

Prior to heading out, the housekeeper sat down in her three-room flat, bathing in despondency while entertaining a sandwich, chewing slow, wondering if life had given her all it could offer or if Mildred was one of the unlucky ones. Her fingers traced the edge of her chipped mug as she stared at the clock, her sigh heavy and drawn out, the ticking second hand mirroring the slow passage of her own fleeting hope.

★ ★ ★

Silas Mercer didn't appreciate Ogden, Utah. Too cold, too far from Los Angeles. He wasn't here for the scenery, and he wasn't staying long. Best to get it done and go quickly.

Mercer dressed like a man who didn't have a choice—wrinkled black pants, a white shirt gone soft with wear, an old hat tugged low, and a windbreaker that hung loosely on his out-of-shape frame. He'd spring for better clothes if better clothes didn't cost dough.

Asking around town wasn't difficult. Locals gabbed when you understood how to listen. He figured no one up here knew him anyhow. A cab took him up into the hills, where, beyond a dirt driveway, the house sat back from the road. Stately once, sagging now, barely grasping its former grandeur. Neglected, it mirrored the bygone silent movie star who had clung to it since moving here in '33.

"Too easy," he muttered confidently, approaching the steps.

He rapped on the weathered wood, waited only a beat, and, without a modicum of patience, rapped again.

Two minutes crawled by, patience wearing thin. Then, a shadow shifted betwixt the curtains. Its owner appeared—that unyielding, ruthless visage from twenty years ago.

Lila gaped the door. "I'm expecting my maid," she said haughtily.

That voice, high and squeaky; he recalled it now. It seeped into his entrails like poison.

He kept it together, his peepers contemptuously sweeping over her, taking in the slacks. He'd always hated a woman in slacks.

"I'm here," he lied humbly, standing straight as a cadet, "for the chauffeur job."

There was anger in her eyes; not recognition, just vexation at the stranger's encroachment. "Got one!" she barked, shoving the door shut. "Good day!"

Lucky for him, his foot was already atop the threshold. The door bounced off his scuffed black shoe. He drove it open with a sharp kick and lunged inside.

She spun to run. He was faster.

By the time he tackled her from behind in the

hallway, he had one of his fine lady Ruby's nylons balled tight in his left pocket.

Lila Varnay's last words were a strangled gasp. "I have money."

The killer sneered grimly. "No, you don't."

She lay prone beneath him as he straddled her posterior, mirroring a rodeo rider, the nylon garrote biting savagely. He yanked it taut, wrenching her cranium upward.

"You didn't...recognize me," he hollered in between breaths. "Silas Mercer!"

It was over in an instant. Her face darkened to purple. His burned red, compliments of the effort.

⋆   ⋆   ⋆

Mildred, the maid, appeared in the affluent neighborhood minutes later, lugging a bucket of cleaning supplies. The sun hit her mid-forties skin like it was trying to remind her she wasn't youthful anymore. As she trudged up the hill, she couldn't help but ponder: how did two women, both nearly the exact same age, end up so far apart in life?

Right before Miss Varnay's driveway, Mildred spotted a scruffy man scuttling along the street toward her, his head low. It was a tranquil area. Fortunately for him, he flagged down a lone cabbie about a hundred feet away from her. She paid it no mind.

The housecleaner continued. The manor's entrance

was ajar; however, it didn't startle her until she ventured indoors and saw Lila Varnay's corpse.

The scream tore out of her—"Ahhhh!"—but she quickly smothered it, using spindly, trembling fingers.

Mildred egressed the house, a murder on her mind. A few blocks down the incline, she fetched her own cab. She had a hunch the man she hardly saw—Mr. Scruffy, unbeknownst to her, Silas Mercer— was bound for the train station.

Once Mildred arrived, she witnessed the stranger boarding a train for Los Angeles. The cleaning lady couldn't fathom why Mr. Scruffy killed the actress. Frankly, she didn't care. He wasn't returning in a hurry, she figured, spying him disappear into the railcar.

The twisted idea came fast—too fast—but it stuck.

Back at the dilapidated, majestic dwelling, with determination set in stone, she wrapped her arms around the lifeless body, its warmth already fading. For the next thirty minutes, she pulled it in short spurts inside the old barn beyond the home.

* * *

That night, Mildred stayed put, helped herself unabashedly to the pantry, and slept well in a sumptuous bed crafted for a queen.

The subsequent afternoon, the housekeeper tugged her collar up against the crisp Utah air, then briskly walked the three blocks to the drugstore. The joint smelled of camphor and hair tonic. The clerk barely peered up from his newspaper when she asked for Egyptian Henna, auburn.

At the residence, Mildred carefully mixed the powder with hot water, watching it turn into a gooey, earthy paste. She methodically worked the henna through the tresses, her fingers steady, the product leaving traces on her skin as she encircled her dome in a towel, and let time stew.

While she waited, she explored the vanity drawer. Lila Varnay's life on paper: passports, a checkbook, various membership cards, charge plates, a stack of twenties. Most important was a driver's license.

An hour later, she vigorously rinsed the dye, dried her locks, and garbed herself in a borrowed emerald green, soft-collar sheath dress featuring mother-of-pearl buttons plus a sash belt. Gawking in the mirror, she smirked. Mildred was gone. Lila Varnay was reborn, like a stranger slipping into a new skin she could easily get used to.

At 2 p.m., Walter Henshaw knocked on the door. Mildred had crossed paths with the old chauffeur on several occasions; he was a fixture around the place. However, knowing firsthand that Lila never had visitors, Henshaw was the only obstacle standing in her way.

She deftly slipped a pre-written note and a twenty-dollar bill into the mail slot.

Walter,

   I will no longer be requiring your services.
Funds are low.
   Thank you, and please push the car keys
inside the slot.
   Miss Varnay

Hours passed. The imposter eased the Rolls-Royce into the lot of a used car dealer on 24th Street. The man took one glance at the fine leather seats and practically licked his lips.

She left with a '39 Ford, plus a small stack of bills—a bad deal for her but a perfect one for staying out of sight.

The imposter drove west, waiting for full dark.

In the rear of a shuttered service station, Mildred hauled and plopped an empty oil drum inside the trunk. It clanged as she set it down, but no one heard. No one cared.

Back at the house, the earth beyond the old barn was soft due to recent rain. Employing a lantern and a shovel, Mildred dug until the moon hit its zenith, then arduously dragged Lila's shell from the barn. It wasn't easy; it was stiff, dead weight now.

The makeshift coffin barrel was dropped unceremoniously into the hole first, followed by the corpse. She closed the lid, then hastily poured dirt in after it.

She needed a shower.

⋆ ⋆ ⋆

A day later, Mildred slid behind the wheel of the Ford, its inconspicuous nature serving its purpose. She traveled south, forty miles on Route 89, to Zions Bank & Trust Company in Salt Lake City, the gravelly hum of the engine vibrating under her guidance. A gut instinct told her Lila loathed populated areas and wouldn't be known in this institution outside of the newspapers.

The counterfeit debutante stepped out, clad in a fitted crepe dress, its waist cinched tight by a narrow belt. The high neckline curved into a subtle bateau contour, while on the backside a row of covered buttons ran down more for show than practical use. She wore a wide-brimmed hat and gigantic sunglasses, shielding her orbs—a phantom of old Hollywood gliding through the present. The new Lila Varnay didn't require Ole' Henshaw's assistance.

Inside the bank, the marble floors gleamed beneath the buzz of industrial lights. Mildred strutted to the counter, exhibiting intent, her heels clicking against the stone. The young female teller gazed up, offering a quirky smile. Mildred gave a polite nod, sliding the checkbook across the counter naturally.

"I want to withdraw two hundred dollars from my account," she instructed, her speech shaped into a manufactured warble—Lila's, not Mildred's. The employee glanced at the name on the record, her

brows knitting slightly, as if it sounded familiar, then smoothed her expression and nodded, pulling a ledger closer and reaching for a pen.

Mildred's heart raced, but she kept her face cool, remembering the woman she was pretending to be. The teller forked over ten Andrew Jacksons, neatly stacked and counted. Mildred guided them into her unscrupulously claimed maroon leather purse.

A new life—Lila's life—had just begun, or so she thought, oblivious to the hushed snap of a newspaper shutterbug's camera, oblivious to the danger.

* * *

The woman, Ruby, who'd lived an existence on lung-burners and bad decisions, lackadaisically sprawled across the divan, one nyloned leg draped over an armrest, a cig idly smoldering between two painted talons. The *Hollywood Citizen-News* lay splayed on her lap, the headline popping her lids amid a haze of bluish vapor. She let out a hollow chuckle, exuding an air of confidence, then tapped ash into an empty highball glass.

"Hey, Silas," she called over her shoulder, "have you seen my jewelry?"

"Nope. Goin' somewhere?"

"Nah." She reread the headline, making sure her foggy mind had it right. "Hey, babe, get a load of this!"

Across the dimly lit parlor, Mr. Mercer didn't look

up. He was bent over a bottle of whiskey, the lines in his phiz carved deep with wear, courtesy of too many unforgiving years.

Ruby smirked and read aloud, stretching out the words as though she were savoring every syllable. "'Down to Earth Lila Varnay—Drives Ford, Gives Autographs to Fans.' Imagine that, honey. Your gone girl's signin' playbills and cruisin' around in some jalopy."

The air in their quarters grew heavier, courtesy of tension, teetering on the edge of bedlam.

Silas lifted his head slowly, dark eyes narrowing. He snatched the goods from her hands, his heart fluttering as he scanned the print.

"No," he muttered. His fingers curled tight into the margins, ruffling the cheap newsprint. He examined it again, the words blurring in his vision. *I drained the existence out of her,* he mused dangerously. *Has to be dead.*

Ruby puffed. Their facial expressions crossed. She knew it was time to listen; her input would do little to assuage the brewing storm in Silas Mercer.

The temperature felt hotter. "Alive?" he blurted.

"Appears you got some unfinished business, lover," she purred cautiously.

Silas stood, the chair scraping against frayed tiles. His kisser was granite, but his grip on the paper shook.

"How could she," he questioned, pounding the shabby table, "survive my attack?"

Ruby inhaled another drag and unhurriedly exhaled fumes toward the ceiling. "Either you didn't pull hard enough...or ghosts know how to operate Fords these days."

★   ★   ★

At 6:45 p.m., the train rumbled to a stop in Ogden, its engine humming low as passengers spilled out into the chill of an early evening. Among them, two men disembarked without exchanging a glance at each other. They had shared the same ride from Los Angeles, breathing the same stale air, but they might as well have been worlds apart.

Silas Mercer, broadcasting his devious, weathered, unsmiling mug and a jacket crumpled due to never finding a hanger, slipped covertly into the shadows where the dusk stretched endlessly, slithering in a deterministic conviction.

Paradoxically, the second man walked with the confidence of someone who expected the world to step aside. His gray suit was pressed sharp, his shoes polished clean, and his fedora sat tilted perfectly. He carried himself like a man accustomed to top-shelf liquor and quiet brothels. The initial neon hum of twilight led him to a barroom; he settled on a stool estranged from the other patrons.

Outside, the sky faded from bruised purple to

black. In an alley blocks away, Silas Mercer—the man Mildred coined Mr. Scruffy—dallied, his paws nestled in his coat pockets, watching the town blink to life. The ebony hours were advancing, along with whatever business had brought both men, unfamiliar with one another, here.

A lazy saxophone moaned out of the jukebox, melancholy in its tune, fighting for space amid the low murmur of conversation. Smoke eddied below the ceiling lamps, ghosts having nowhere to go. The bar had seen healthier days, but like Silas Mercer, the debonair newcomer wasn't going to be in Ogden long. He eased off his hat, setting it on the vacant stool beside him, as if reserving the spot for something better.

A pretty, mid-twenties brunette slid his direction, wiping a glass with a rag. Her voice aired rough, like gravel under tires. "What'll it be, stranger?"

The gentleman angled his torso just enough to let the overhead glow catch his features; he was double her age. She took him in deliberately, studying his blonde hair, combed just right, sculpted face, dimpled chin, and blue eyes.

"I go by Gordon. Gordon Rockford." He broadcast it as though he expected the lounge to gasp. "Gimme a Manhattan. Keep 'em coming."

She shrugged at the unfamiliar name, poured the cocktail, and slid it his way. The first two, she made proper. The subsequent two got friendlier with the ice. The more he drank, the less she fancied him.

As the bar became busier, a skinny man snagged the stool next to Mr. Rockford, plenty close to catch whatever nonsense spilled out of his lips.

The bartender leaned on the counter. "So, what's a big shot like you doing in Ogden?"

Mr. Rockford swirled his glass, observing the amber ripple. "Keeping an eye on my money."

Her brow ticked up. "That so?"

"You know Lila Varnay?" he asked, his words now slurring a bit.

She smirked. "Everyone's heard of her. Nobody knows her. Doesn't mingle among the locals."

"Well," he divulged, "I'm her attorney, maybe her only friend. Need to chug a few down the hole before I visit her; dame's high-hat."

She let out a delicate laugh. "I guess I understand. Takes gumption."

Rockford's fingers drummed the bar. "Haven't heard from her in over a week. Usually writes every couple of days. Rumor is she's getting careless with what's remaining of her savings."

"Mrs. Varnay earned it," the bartender said, fixing him an additional, watered-down drink.

"Possibly. But something's not right."

She drifted off to tend another customer. The thin man on the next stool finally spoke, his voice low and smooth. "Just a heads-up, pal. The frail," he jerked his chin toward her, "she's Detective Larson's daughter."

Rockford exhaled sluggishly and measured him up. "That supposed to mean more than squat to me?"

The man smiled. "Depends," he responded, pitching an air of incivility, "on how much trouble you're looking for."

★   ★   ★

Same evening, 8 p.m. in a smoky room off a corridor at the Ogden police station, fifty-four-year-old Detective Larson set the receiver back in its cradle with a slow, wary motion, his hairy fingers lingering on the Bakelite for a second longer than necessary. A cigarette dangled loosely between rectangular lips.

His hazel eyes squinted, set in a once handsome, now battle-worn visage, which had received more hits from the job than from fists. A square chin gave him the impression of a man who could take a punch and return one twice as hard. He possessed a decent mop of ashen hair that hadn't seen a comb since breakfast.

Larson wasn't fat, but certainly not in shape. His dark suit hung on him like a second skin, creased and rumpled ubiquitously.

A loosened, wrinkled tie draped his collar, mimicking a noose.

Across the office, Detective Holt, a much younger, fitter individual than Larson, leaned over a smaller desk, pupils scanning a notepad, bearing the kind of focus which belonged to men who still believed in things. His red coif was neatly combed, though thinning spots had begun creeping along the temples. The green dick's face hadn't seen sufficient misfortune yet. Give it time, Larson, his mentor, frequently assured him.

Unexpectedly, an ancient desk sergeant ushered in a well-dressed, diminutive man, pushing sixty, and instructed him to sit in an wooden chair not built for comfort. It appeared the last year the visitor had a strand growing on the top of his skull was when Charles Lindbergh was flying the *Spirit of St. Louis* over the Atlantic.

Detective Larson recognized the man in the adjacent seat as Harry Cohen, president of the Ogden branch of Zions Bank & Trust Company, a well-respected financial pillar of the community.

Larson knew him well enough to refer to him by his first name. "What can we do for you, Harry?"

In the background, Holt tuned in.

"Lila Varnay brings me here."

"Go on."

"You see," said the pint-sized man, supinating a palm, "she's exhibiting odd behavior. Signs autographs, and drives all the way south to our Salt Lake branch to make withdrawals. And it seems like every day. Also, she's doing it in a Ford; very atypical of her."

Larson felt a flicker of zeal—he lived for moments

when work veered an interesting turn—but his inflection stayed neutral. "I agree. Sounds a bit peculiar."

"Yes, and according to the teller who reported it, she's penning her signature using her right hand."

"And?" Larson figured he already knew the answer to the question.

"Lila Varnay," Mr. Cohen divulged to Larson unsurprisingly, "is left-handed."

"Well, Harry, I just got off the phone with my daughter. She served drinks to a possible swindler from Cali at Louie's bar tonight. The fiend called Varnay's money 'my money.' This whole scenario is suspicious."

"I see. And bet his name is Gordon Rockford; a fellow who is overly involved in Miss Varnay's affairs."

"Yep. Is Varnay loaded?" asked Larson, fervently milling his cigarette.

"Not so much anymore. The ex-actress lives off interest on her remaining funds."

"Why does he call it 'my money'?"

"He is her attorney and, for ages, has been trying to coerce her into making him sole beneficiary to all she has left." The banker scratched his bald head and made known, "She has no such intentions."

"Go figure," Larson quipped, his tone ornery. He then added, "Keep mum for now, Harry."

After the financier exited, Larson turned to his partner. "Let's grab our hats and get movin'. There's one person who will know more."

It was a rundown shack on the outskirts of town. Walter Henshaw, his white hair a messy halo encircling his head, opened the door, already in his pajamas. He told Detectives Larson and Holt his story about the termination note.

Detective Larson nodded attentively.

To the senior citizen, the younger Detective Holt probed, "What else can you tell us?"

"Well...Miss Varnay wouldn't drive a Ford or any other car," Henshaw muttered, his tone flat as a brothel mattress underneath a four-hundred-pound man on payday. "Doubt she can even drive. Might have a license, though, I reckon. Told me once."

The coppers exchanged a glance, meticulously weighing the details. They were about to turn and walk out when Henshaw spoke again.

"Hey, hold on," he said, his voice low but grimly certain. "It's Thursday night. If it's really Miss Varnay, she'll be leavin' her villa at ten. Thursdays, she always does a late dinner at The Golden Lantern after the crowd's thinned out. I know her schedule by heart."

Larson peered at his watch, then shot Holt a look. "It's quarter past nine. Let's move."

★   ★   ★

At 9:40 p.m., Silas Mercer donned black gloves and stepped into the barn behind the residence. The structure smelled of expired hay and weathered wood, its rafters groaning under the weight of time, its contents cluttered like an eighty-year-old man's junk shop.

The Ford in the driveway told him his nemesis was home. He flicked his cigarette lighter, its weak flame casting jittery outlines in the periphery, merely enough to see.

An axe wasn't difficult to find. But in the dark, his grip closed around another object, something he wasn't searching for—a crowbar. He grinned. Now, he had two accoutrements.

He discovered an additional surprise. Beyond the barn, the woods yielded into a clearing, a trail leading downhill. A ready-made escape route back to town. Convenient.

Satisfied he had a getaway, it was now time for the intrusion. At the rear of the crumbling château, he employed the crowbar, methodically working at the cellar window frame with small, effortless yanks until it loosened. He slid it out and leaned it against the foundation. He ditched the crowbar, laid the axe near the opening, and shimmied himself to the cement floor.

He reached up for the weapon of choice, and his phalanges curled around its handle. He inspected the blade, then whispered, *"You won't survive this one, bitch."*

Silas Mercer surreptitiously crept up the cellar stairs. The door was unlocked. Convenient.

The dwelling held its breath. He glided stealthily, his footsteps ghosts upon the floorboards. In the hallway, he perceived the low rhythm of snoring. The same hallway where he'd killed Lila Varnay a little over a week ago.

"*Already asleep?*" He chuckled darkly.

The portal to the bedroom eased open under his touch. The snoring thickened. The only illumination came via a sliver of moonlight cutting through the panes. He saw her hair.

Easy target, his mind told him.

As he inched closer, he took in her strident respirations. She was lying prone. Convenient.

Aiming at her cervical spine, he viciously swung twice—once for death, once for good riddance. In between chops, he heard a stark, startled gasp, cut off almost instantly. Then the head hit the floor with a dull thud. Mr. Scruffy gave it a shove, jutting his shoe, sending it into the shadows for a one-point goal.

On the pillow, something glimmered—a necklace. He plucked it up, dropped it into his palm, then slipped it into his pocket. Another trip to the pawn shop couldn't hurt.

For a few seconds, he lingered, motionless, reminiscing about how, twenty years ago, Lila Varnay's wrath had sent him into a life of crime. No choice, no way out.

Just as Mercer was about to turn the pad over for anything worth taking, a movement in the front window stopped him cold. Across the street, an unmarked car with two passengers crept to a halt. The headlights went out.

His stomach ominously murmured, *Fuzz.*

He didn't wait to be sure. He bolted out the rear door and hit the trail in the woods, running.

From the driver's seat, Larson spied Mildred's Ford in the driveway. He rotated his wrist, checking his timepiece.

"If she doesn't come out by ten, we knock," he said to Holt.

At 9:55 p.m., a cab rolled up. A man stumbled out, swaying on unsteady legs, too intoxicated to notice the undercovers in the Chevrolet. He weaved up the driveway, showcasing the kind of jaunt that reeked of booze.

"That's gotta be Gordon...whatever his last name is," Holt muttered

"Rockford," Larson corrected. "You'll learn to remember those things, kid."

*   *   *

Gordon Rockford hammered relentlessly on the peeled wooden door, each blow landing with a flat thud. No answer. He circled left, moving along the side of the Varnay house, slipping out of sight of Detectives Larson and Holt, who sat cooling their heels in the Chevy.

Around back, Mr. Rockford encountered the removed cellar window. He shouted into the opening,

"Lila, Lila?" The dapper visitor tossed his suit jacket onto the surrounding cement and grudgingly squeezed his bulk through, landing in the dark. He journeyed the abyss, expecting to find the worst.

Sixty seconds later, the bedroom ceiling light buzzed bright, revealing the horror sprawled on the bed: a headless husk. A butchered woman.

"Lila! Nooo!" The name tore raggedly out of him as he staggered hindward, clutching his gut. He desperately bolted for the bathroom and vomited profusely, spilling his guts into the porcelain all-purpose bowl some people call the crapper. The secretions came again and again until there was nothing left but dry heaves and cold sweat. He splashed water on his face and tried to steady the shaking in his upper extremities.

The phone sat within reach. He seized the receiver. "Operator, get me—"

Then Mr. Rockford saw the rear porch entry, Silas Mercer's exit, wide open, yawning, resembling a trap. His breathing paused. He slammed the receiver down and locked the door. No cops. No sirens. Solely him, alone, in a place he had no business being.

At that exact instant, the lawmen were on the move. In the thick of the murk, Larson's keen eye caught the jimmied window. He took charge and nudged Holt. "Here's how he entered. You take the basement. I'll cut around front."

Holt obeyed. Meanwhile, Larson slunk across

the gloom toward the dwelling's anterior, remaining outside, and gawked through the glass, mirroring a Peeping Tom hunting for a dame in lingerie.

Gordon Rockford's fingers feverishly started exploring the vanity. In the drawer, stacks of crisp greenbacks stared at him.

His mind was distorted from alcohol, discovering a corpse, and greed. He located a compact suitcase and started stuffing it with whatever his pilfering hands could grab—cash, jewels, anything that glittered.

Shrouded in shadows, Detective Larson watched through the glass, dumbstruck, breath caught in his chest.

Meanwhile, Holt tiptoed along the undercroft, moving quietly, gun drawn.

Mr. Rockford had barely passed the front entrance threshold when Holt struck. A hard grip seized his posterior, followed by a sharp yank, and Gordon Rockford went down swiftly. The suitcase flew from his grasp, bursting open as it hit the ground, a fortune scattering onto the damp lawn.

Larson stepped up, snapping the cuffs on Rockford's wrists with glacial detachment. He jerked his noggin at Holt. "Phone headquarters. And start looking around. I got a notion we're standing on a stiff."

Mr. Rockford thrashed wildly. "No! No," he choked. "You have it all wrong!"

But the night wasn't listening.

★   ★   ★

Back in Los Angeles, in the same dingy apartment, Silas Mercer sat at a kitchen table with three good legs—the wobbly fourth a makeshift prop straight out of a two-bit picture—hunched over a salami sandwich, picking at it like he knew it was stale.

The door swung open, letting in Ruby—his favorite biscuit, for now. She sauntered in and dropped the morning paper, a flap echoing in the stillness.

VELVET SHADOWS STAR LILA VARNAY AND MAID FOUND DEAD IN UTAH—LAWYER GORDON ROCKFORD PINCHED FOR DOUBLE MURDER

The subhead spelled it out plain: *DA Alleges Los Angeles Attorney Rockford Iced Varnay with Help from an Ogden Housekeeper Who Later Assumed Her Identity—Double-Cross Ends in Blood." The twist? "Once the lady skimmed enough loot, Rockford cut her out of the act—permanently.*

Silas Mercer studied the print. A slow, wicked grin spread across his face. Convenient.

For updates on this writer's work, follow him on Facebook: Allan Kevorkian, Noir and Pulp Fiction Author.

WHERE DID THE IDEAS FOR THESE STORIES COME FROM?

First of all, you have to dig deep into your imagination. Every story begins with a spark—sometimes a fleeting image, a quick glimpse, or a sudden thought that refuses to let go. Like a painter after applying the initial stroke, you follow your gut intuition and see where it leads.

Free Lunch and a Hundred Bucks—I just had an image of two people meeting for lunch by accident, and I let the typewriter keys do the rest. The dog track scene is a memory of our now-defunct Lincoln Greyhound Park—watching the gamblers, their expressions so intense. The cliff scene was derived from several of those great film noir movies I watched as a kid.

The Books—The character Mike is a twisted take on my grandfather, Michael Vescera. My fictitious story is based on a true story he told me as a kid—about the time some local wise guys from the old neighborhood wanted to store some underworld books in his shop's basement. He refused, and nothing ever really came of it. If he were still alive, he'd probably take me over his knee. He certainly never killed anyone, never hid sinister secrets, and he wasn't a widower. In truth, he was a gentleman, just as you see him earlier in the story. He was a U.S. Navy torpedo man in the Pacific during WWII and a well-known local theatre artist in the city of Providence.

Papa, as we called him, did have a shop just around the corner from the Loew's State Theatre. As a kid, I remember it as a special place filled with his works from years past. My favorite was an Allen Freed Rock 'n' Roll concert poster he designed. By the 1970s, the rise of lower-cost screen printing hurt his business. And yes, kids from RISD did frequent his shop.

Last Day—This story sprang from a moment in my life that's hard to forget. At twenty, I was working in New Jersey for a traveling salesman-slash-marketing outfit—strictly 100 percent commission. A friend from back home in Rhode Island had joined me for the hustle. Our gig involved dropping off brochures advertising microwave containers at local businesses. If someone placed an order, we'd deliver it the next day and get paid.

Thinking big, we targeted a hospital somewhere down Jersey Shore, south of Perth Amboy. We blanketed every employee breakroom we could find with our brochures. Halfway through, security caught wind and kicked us out, warning us never to return. But by the next day, we had several orders from hospital employees.

That's when things went sideways.

We had someone new shadowing us, and figured it'd be a bright idea to send her—driving my car—to make those deliveries while we waited across the street in a supermarket. So, we waited. And waited. She never came back. Either she'd stolen the car and the goods, or something had gone wrong at the hospital. Right as that uneasy thought struck me, four police cruisers screeched up outside, lights spinning, sirens blaring. I knew they were for us. My friend and I tugged our hats low, pretending to be shoppers.

I'll never forget those last few minutes of freedom—that strange clarity you feel when you know the bluecoats are coming for you. That sensation became the engine behind the story.

Oh—and our real ending? After getting fingerprinted and tossed in a cell, I made my one phone call. Lucky for me, it was a lottery ticket. The hospital dropped the trespassing charges within the hour. An overreaction—on their part.

Man Next Door—My dad became the "old man" next door in his Providence, Rhode Island neighborhood, having lived in the same house from 1950 to 2018, except for a six-year break during his brief marriage to my mother. He stubbornly insisted on living alone in his final years, even as dementia took hold. He saw the neighborhood change around him and, like the man next door, kept makeshift weapons under his bed and hoarded piles of goods in several rooms. Yes, he claimed people were breaking in to steal his food, and he really did believe the intruders possessed the strange contraption mentioned in the story. In his later years, Dad kept to himself. He had a stint in the army and was always the kind of man waiting for action. He would've come to Ruth's aid just as the character did at the end of this tale.

Two Birds, One Stone—The storyline takes place two months before my first novel, *No Escape from Death*, so it serves as a kind of prequel. I plan on writing another full-length Max Weatherbee story in the future, and wanted to stay connected to how I write him—and Johnny Knuckles. The character of Johnny Knuckles holds a special place in my heart; he originates from one of my teenage friends who passed away young.

They Won't Hurt You—I hadn't planned on writing a ghost story. But my wife and I recently visited a place in Vermont called Wilson Castle. It's a fascinating place—look it up. One of the tour guides showed us photos on her phone that various visitors had taken over the years. In some of them, you can see tourists posing, but in the background—reflected in mirrors—there appear to be faint, ghostly figures in late 1880s garb. Are mirrors portals to their world?

Do ghosts really exist? Are they just the result of overlapping dimensions in time? I have no idea—and no plans to spend a night there to find out! Still, the idea worked its way into a noir setting nicely. And remember: the ghosts themselves didn't do any of the killing in this story.

Bus Driver—The whole idea for the tale didn't start with the bus driver. It began with a story my dad once told me about a man who used to terrorize his friend's apartment complex back when they were teenagers, in the early 1950s. A menacing presence in the corridors—someone everyone was afraid to encounter. They nicknamed him Coyote. Supposedly, he worked as a leg breaker for a local loan shark, and I doubt anyone in the building would have argued with that.

My dad's uncle Aram used to take him down into a dank cellar to teach him how to box. And when I was a kid, Dad showed me the best way to deal with bullies—an open-hand chop to the nose. My dad often talked about a Moondog radio music show he used to listen to. All those memories filtered into the story.

Breadbasket—I just had a vision of a man and his wife after an argument, and him following a cab with the wrong person in it. Everything else before and after just came to mind as I typed.

Blood on His Hands—The Allentown-Bethlehem area is special to me. I worked out there for a few months when I was around twenty. Even back then, I remember how much I enjoyed checking out old buildings, especially state hospitals. We have a similar site here in Rhode Island, home to a lesser-traveled road with no posted speed limit, where folks often drive fast. There are no sidewalks, and yes, it's common to see vagrants walking along it. I also wanted to bring in an Armenian lead character. So, I put it all together, and a tale was formed—a twisted one!

Silent Movie Star—My wife and I visited Ogden, Utah, in 2022. Lovely place! It has a well-preserved vintage train station that's been converted into a museum. While we were there, we found out that Ben Lomond Peak, located just north of Ogden, is believed to have inspired the original Paramount Pictures logo. That sparked the idea of a former silent movie star hiding out in the area, and the rest developed into something very sinister.

ACKNOWLEDGMENTS

I would like to thank the following:

- My beta readers—sons Allan Kazar and Bedros, Jeff Tracy, Jennifer Kevorkian, children's book author Linda Marie (Abbruzzese), and Patty Mariani—for taking the time to read these stories and offer thoughtful feedback.

- Everyone who purchased my first book, *No Escape from Death*, and encouraged me to write another.

- My late father, Allan Kevorkian Sr., who introduced me to film noir movies and pulp fiction reading at a young age.

- My wife, Jennifer Kevorkian, who persuaded me to return to my writing hobby after I'd left it behind during my late mother's illness.

- Steven and Dawn Porter of Stillwater River Publications, for making my dream possible.

- The folks at Wilson Castle in Vermont—if not for that visit, I wouldn't have come up with the idea for *They Won't Hurt You.*

- All the film noir and vintage pulp fiction fans out there—without you, I wouldn't have had the motivation to pen these stories. I knew you'd appreciate them the most.

ABOUT THE AUTHOR

 Allan, a native Rhode Islander, has always been a big fan of film noir and vintage pulp fiction stories. His ethnic background is Armenian and Italian, which he enjoys incorporating into many of his characters. Allan has worked as an RN for most of his adult life but recently decided to try his hand at writing noir stories. His first two books, *No Escape from Death* and *10 Twisted Pulp Fiction Tales*, are heavily influenced by classic film noir movies and pulp writers such as Richard Stark, Cornell Woolrich, Raymond Chandler, Harold Masur, Dashiell Hammett, Mickey Spillane, and the many stories featured in *Black Mask*. Allan puts his own touch in all his work, including some fresh humor along the way.

In his free time, Allan enjoys exploring off-the-beaten-path places in small-town USA, hitting the gym, and going on moderate hikes. During family vacations with his wife and two sons, he organizes a pseudo murder mystery, assigning hotel staff as suspects and giving them each a character name. At the end of the trip, the family votes to decide, "Who did it?"

www.ingramcontent.com/pod-product-compliance
Lightning Source LLC
Chambersburg PA
CBHW061518020726
47502CB00006B/2126